Getting A Mommy Is A Really Big Job.

I'm not complaining, though, 'cuz Daddy really appreciates all the help I've been giving him. He says that if it weren't for me, his life would be dull and boring!

Operation Mommy is going great. With my help, Daddy and Shay have been together every day and I can tell they like each other from all the nice things they say. Yesterday, Daddy told Shay that for a lady who didn't have any little kids of her own, she sure knew a lot! And Shay told Daddy he could stop pretending to be perfect any time he wanted to.

I wish they'd hurry up and decide to get married....

Dear Reader,

Here at Desire, hot summer months mean even *hotter* reading, beginning with Joan Johnston's *The Disobedient Bride*, the next addition to her fabulous Children of Hawk's Way series—*and* July's *Man of the Month*.

Next up is *Falcon's Lair*, a sizzling love story by Sara Orwig, an author many of you already know—although she's new to Desire. And if you like family stories, don't miss Christine Rimmer's unforgettable *Cat's Cradle or* Caroline Cross's delightful *Operation Mommy*.

A book from award winner Helen R. Myers is always a treat, so I'm glad we have *The Rebel and the Hero* this month. And Diana Mars's many fans will be thrilled with *Mixed-up Matrimony*. If you like humor, you'll like this engaging—and *very* sensuous—love story.

Next month, there is much more to look forward to, including *The Wilde Bunch*, a *Man of the Month* by Barbara Boswell, and *Heart of the Hunter*, the first book in a new series by BJ James.

As always, your opinions are important to me. So continue to let me know what you like about Silhouette Desire!

Sincerely,

Lucia Macro
Senior Editor

Please address questions and book requests to:
Silhouette Reader Service
U.S.: 3010 Walden Ave., P.O. Box 1325, Buffalo, NY 14269
Canadian: P.O. Box 609, Fort Erie, Ont. L2A 5X3

CAROLINE
CROSS
OPERATION MOMMY

SILHOUETTE *Desire*®
Published by Silhouette Books
America's Publisher of Contemporary Romance

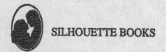

SILHOUETTE BOOKS

ISBN 0-373-05939-6

OPERATION MOMMY

Copyright © 1995 by Jen M. Heaton

Printed in U.S.A.

Books by Caroline Cross

Silhouette Desire

Dangerous #810
Rafferty's Angel #851
Truth or Dare #910
Operation Mommy #939

CAROLINE CROSS

always loved to read, but it wasn't until she discovered romance novels that she felt compelled to write, fascinated by the chance to explore the power of love to effect positive change in people's lives. She has since been nominated for several awards and was thrilled to win *Romantic Times'* Reviewer's Choice Award for Best Silhouette Desire of 1993 for *Dangerous*. Caroline grew up in central Washington State, attended the University of Puget Sound and now lives outside Seattle with her husband, two daughters and an ever-changing collection of pets.

To Tim, Jessica and Katy, who gave up *their* summer plans so I could spend mine with Alex, Shay and Brady. And to Sandi and Melinda, who answered the phone— even when they knew it was me. I wouldn't have made it without you.

Prologue

———

Dateline: July 1

To: Beau Morrison
    Correspondent, World News International
        Magazine
    c/o Istanbul News Desk
    Micromini cassette tape No. 1

Hey, Uncle Beau! It's me, your favorite nephew, Brady.
And I bet you can't guess, not in a million, kazillion
years, how come I'm sending this tape to you.

The reason is—I found her! I finally found the most
perfect, awesome mom in the world for me and Nick
and Mikey! And I bet you're gonna be real happy, 'cuz
it's your friend, Shay, who you sent to stay at your
cottage!

She's so cool, Uncle Beau.

You won't believe what happened the first time I met her. The Prune Face—that's our new nanny—invited Shay to come swimming at the pool. And when Shay did, Leonardo, my lizard, crawled into her beach bag to take a little nap.

I'm telling you, Uncle Beau, me and Nick and Mikey waited a trillion years for her to stick her hand in there. And when she finally did, we waited another bazillion for her to scream and stuff.

Only she didn't. She just took out her suntan lotion and leaned back in her chair and said, "Did I tell you boys about the time your uncle and I did a story on the Amazon? The natives there made the best lizard stew. Maybe you'd like to come by the cottage tonight and try some?"

Of course, Mikey started to cry. So then the Prune wanted to know what was going on. Only Shay didn't tell. She just smiled and gave Mikey a hug and told him not to worry. And she told the Prune it was all a mistake and then waited until the Prune wasn't looking to give Leo back.

That's when I knew Shay was *the one*, Uncle Beau. But just to make sure—picking a new mom is a really important job, you know—I've been checking her out.

Guess what? She's *better* than perfect.

She doesn't faint at the sight of blood or get mad if her hair gets wet or her clothes get dirty. She likes dogs, cats, rats and gerbils, and she isn't afraid of snakes or spiders. And she knows *lots* of mom stuff. Like how come your fingers get wrinkled in the bathtub, the difference between a T. rex and a pterodactyl, that chocolate chip cookies make owies feel better and even how to do the Heimlich maneuver! But best of all, she doesn't talk to me or Nick or Mikey like we're dumb little kids, even if sometimes Mikey is one.

I thought about what you said—about how Daddy might not want to get married again. But the thing is,

Uncle Beau, he's never home, so why should he care, anyway? Right now, he's in dumb old Florida buying another resort, and even though we talk on the phone, it's not the same as having him here. Sometimes I don't think he remembers Nick and Mikey are still little kids. I mean, I'm almost nine so I can take care of myself, but *they* need somebody to watch out for them.

That's why I made a plan. I call it Operation Mommy, and I just know it's gonna work. As soon as Mrs. Rosencrantz, our housekeeper, leaves for her vacation, I'm gonna get rid of the Prune so me and Nick and Mikey will be all alone. Shay will have to take care of us then, and Daddy will be so worried he'll come right home. When he gets here I'm gonna have candles and flowers and music, and Shay will have on a real pretty dress. Daddy will think she's beautiful, and be so-o-o glad she took such good care of us, he'll ask her to marry him. And of course she'll say yes!

It's gonna be perfect, only I hope they don't kiss all the time and—

Oops, the Prune is yelling again. She says I need to come *Right this minute.* Maybe she found the green food coloring we put in her face lotion....

I love you, Uncle Beau, only don't tell anybody I said so, 'kay? I promise I'll send another tape soon to tell you how everything goes.

This is me, Brady P. Morrison, signing off.

P.S. I think my birthday—it's August 2, just in case you forgot—would be perfect for the wedding. How about you?

One

Port Sandy, Washington
July 5

"Hey, Shay!" Brady yelled into the clothes hamper. "Guess what?"

Shay Spenser, wedged tightly in the laundry chute several feet below floor level, winced as the boy's cheerful voice echoed around her. "I don't know," she called back. "What?"

"Nick says he can see an ambulance *and* a ladder truck!"

Sure enough, now that Shay listened for it, she could hear the rise of two different approaching sirens.

"We never had a ladder truck before!" Brady declared in excitement, as unconcerned about the broader ramifications of her plight as only an eight-year-old could be. "Isn't it cool?"

Unfortunately, Shay had twenty-two years on the boy and, at the moment, was feeling every one. "Oh, yeah.

Cool." Even as she uttered the words, a horrific vision of hoards of firemen descending on the deluxe, fully remodeled, turn-of-the-century house where she was stuck filled her head. The way her luck was running, her rescuers would probably rappel up the pristine white siding, break out a few leaded-glass windows and use fire axes to chop her free.

Shay stifled a groan. If Alex Morrison, the owner of the house and the boys' father, ever decided to come home from his marathon Florida business trip, he'd probably have her arrested.

But then, it wasn't solely her fault that the simple humanitarian act of trying to retrieve the boys' runaway gerbil from the laundry hamper had landed her in this mess. After all, how could she possibly have known the hamper had a hinged bottom? Or that it opened onto a laundry chute big enough to swallow a person?

She couldn't. Nor, for that matter, would she be in this fix if Alex Morrison were any sort of responsible father. Not only had he been gone on business for six weeks—an eternity in the lives of his three young sons—but two days ago, when the boys' nanny had abruptly quit, *he'd* been too busy to return his own son's phone call informing him of the fact!

While it was true the agency that supplied the nanny had called to apologize for the woman's abrupt departure and to arrange for a temporary replacement until Mr. Morrison could be contacted, Shay was far from appeased. What sort of sorry excuse for a father treated his own kids so indifferently?

"Shay? Is it okay if I go look at the trucks?" Brady asked. "I'll only go as far as the window. I promise."

"Sure. Go for it."

"All right!" The hamper door swished shut above her.

Shay shook her head. During her ten years as a journalist, first as an independent, and more recently for WNI magazine, she'd been pinned down by sniper fire in Beirut, had her Land Rover attacked by a bad-tempered rhino in

Kitgum, and been held hostage briefly by guerrilla forces in
El Salvador. This ought to rate as minor in comparison.

Yet right now it didn't feel like it. Her shins smarted from
where she'd scraped them when she'd slipped, her shoulders ached from being wedged against the metal shaft, and
she was starting to get a headache from being upside down
for too long.

Adding to her misery was the growing evidence that Brutus, the creature responsible for her predicament, seemed to
be getting more agitated as time passed. Although she had
a firm grip on the little creature, his pointy toenails were dug
into her palm, and any second now she expected to feel the
sting of his sharp little teeth, as well. After her years in the
news business, Shay could just imagine the headline:
"Award-winning journalist savaged by rodent in bizarre
accident. Details page 5."

Her friend Beau would probably laugh himself silly and
say this was what happened to misguided journalists who
thought they wanted out of the business. Furthermore, he'd
probably claim that this was why he'd lent her his cottage on
his brother's Puget Sound estate in the first place—so she
could discover for herself how ill-suited she was for "normal" life.

Well, maybe he was right, Shay thought wryly, as a noisy
rush of footsteps sounded overhead. A second later Brady,
Nick and Mikey began to shout, "Up here! We're up here!"

She heard a distant cry of acknowledgement, followed by
the din of booted feet thundering up the stairs and coming
down the hall. She flinched as she pictured the black marks
the firemen's rubber-soled boots would leave on the pale
wood floors and thick carpets...a half second before she
reminded herself to be grateful for small favors.

At least they weren't hacking their way through the walls.

Above her, the tromping stopped and a barrage of questions started.

"Did one of you kids call 911?"

"Where's the injured party?"

"Is your mom or dad home?"

"This better not be a prank!"

"Are you boys here all alone?"

"What's the problem?"

As Shay could've predicted, all three Morrisons tried to answer at once.

"We don't got a mom," Mikey volunteered.

"Brady called. He's the oldest!" Nick declared.

"It's Shay," Brady said urgently. "She's stuck in the laundry chute!"

"Hold on, son. She who?"

"Not she, *Shay!*" Brady corrected, sounding exasperated.

Shay sighed. "Hang in there, Brutus. From the sound of things, it's going to be a while before we're liberated."

"Just make sure they've initialed those lease-reversion clauses when the contracts show up, Helen," Alex Morrison said into the car phone, guiding his sleek silver Mercedes into the divided highway's passing lane to get around a slow-moving tractor-trailer rig. "It's taken six weeks to get them included—I don't want any more delays or screw ups. Have the attorneys go over them, and if everything looks all right, messenger them to me at the house."

"Yes, sir." Helen O'Connell, Alex's longtime secretary, sounded crisp and efficient as usual. "Anything else?"

Alex gave a tired sigh. "I hope not. After the past few weeks, I'm ready for some quiet time at home."

Helen made a commiserating sound. "I trust everything is all right with the boys, then?"

Alex frowned. "Why wouldn't it be?"

"Oh, it's only that when Brady called—"

"Hold on. Brady called? When?"

"Why, day before yesterday." The line crackled briefly as the road dipped. "Don't tell me Whitset didn't give you my message?"

"Whitset? Whitset's wife went into labor two days ago. He fainted in the delivery room and knocked himself silly. When he came to, he barely remembered his name, much less to pass on any messages."

"Oh, dear," Helen said.

"Right," Alex said grimly. "Did Brady mention why he was calling?"

There was a pause before Helen said apologetically, "Well, yes and no. He said there was something about Mrs. Kiltz he needed to tell you."

For an instant Alex's mind was blank and then he swore under his breath. Mrs. Kiltz was the nanny he'd hired right before he left. "*Great.* Did he say what?"

"No, sir. He just asked that you call."

"You didn't hear sirens or anyone screaming, did you?"

He was only half joking, and Helen knew it. "Not this time," she quickly reassured him. "Actually, now that I think about it, he seemed extremely cheerful, so I'm sure it couldn't have been anything too major. I asked if Mrs. Rosencrantz had left for her vacation on schedule, and he said yes. I asked if things were all right with the temp the agency sent to fill in for her, and he said yes. And when I asked how everything else was, why, he laughed and said it was perfect."

"Terrific." Alex's apprehension shot up a notch. The last time Brady had claimed everything was "perfect" had been right before a *Lawrence of Arabia* play set, complete with a genuine Bedouin tent and a pair of very cranky camels, had been delivered to the house.

Purchased at great expense through one of the home shopping channels on Alex's credit card, the play set had been touted as the ultimate educational experience. Heaven knew Alex had certainly learned a lot. He'd learned the true meaning of the phrase "all purchases final." He'd learned that in Port Sandy County, camels were considered exotic pets and that you were hit with a whopping fine if you didn't have the proper permit to keep them. He'd learned that when annoyed, the homely creatures spit. But most of all, he'd learned to be on guard when his eldest son started bandying about the word *perfect*.

"Is that all, sir?"

"Yes. Unless the house has burned down—" he tried to inject a light note into his voice and failed "—I should be in the office sometime next week before I leave for New Mexico. You know the drill—if anything comes up, call."

"Yes, sir. And don't worry. I'm sure everything is fine with the boys."

"Right. See you next week." Alex disconnected, waited for a dial tone, then punched his home number on the speed dial at the same time he slowed the Mercedes for his exit.

He turned west at the bottom of the ramp and headed into the late-afternoon sun, grateful for the car's air conditioning. He listened impatiently as the phone began to ring. He was too tired for this right now, he thought. When he had gone to Aristo Cay Resort at the end of May, he'd never expected to be there six weeks. After negotiating its purchase from the Carlyle family for months prior to his arrival, he'd been confident the deal was set and all that was left to do was fine-tune the agreement.

A major miscalculation on his part. But then, there was no way he could have known that Hiram Carlyle's only daughter, Miranda, had recently divorced. Or that she would take one look at him and get it into her head that a temporary merger should be a condition of the sale.

Alex grimaced. Although he hadn't lived like a monk in the four years he'd been widowed, he had made it a firm rule not to mix sex with either his business or family life.

Where his family was concerned, his reasoning was simple. His sons had already lost their mother. No matter what it took, he was determined to protect them from such heartbreak in the future. Since he knew he'd never remarry, there was no reason to involve the boys with women he knew would never be more than casual companions.

Professionally, it was simply a sound business practice. He was thirty-five, unmarried, and CEO of Morrison Retreats, which owned and operated five small, exclusive resorts spread across the United States. The business had been his salvation after his wife died, and he wasn't about to jeopardize it for anything as fleeting as physical pleasure.

Convincing Miranda Carlyle of that, however, had taken a while.

On the other end of the line, the phone continued to ring. Where the heck was everyone? Even if the nanny was tied up with the boys—or the boys had tied her up, which had actually happened a few sitters ago, the housekeeper, temp or not, ought to answer.

Unless something had happened. Unless—

Alex took a deep breath, then slowly exhaled. *Knock it off. Just because no one's answering the phone doesn't mean something has happened.* More likely the housekeeper was vacuuming and didn't hear the phone, and Mrs. Kiltz and the boys were taking a nature walk or something.

Except that Brady had told Helen there was a problem.

Alex ground his teeth against an urge to curse. He jerked the phone away from his ear, thought for a moment, hit the disconnect button and again pressed the speed dial. Once more the phone began to ring, although a quick glance at the dashboard clock, which read half past five, made it unlikely this call would be answered, either.

Two rings later there was a click on the line, and a recorded voice said cheerfully, "You have reached Aunt Frannie's Nannys, quality domestic caregivers for young and old. We are not in at the moment, but if you'd like to leave a message, we'll be happy to return your call."

Scowling, Alex left his name and number. He turned south onto the dead-end road that led to his house above the coast, switched on the radio and tried to forget about everything but getting home as fast as possible. Pressing on the accelerator, he felt a grim satisfaction as the sleek sedan surged forward, only to have his stomach plummet some ten minutes later when he approached his driveway and found the electronically operated gate wide open.

Gripping the steering wheel so hard his knuckles turned white, he stomped on the gas petal and shot through the opening, oblivious to the bright splashes of magenta, rose and crimson from the late-blooming rhododendrons that lined the long circular drive.

It took what felt like hours before he rounded the final curve. The house rose up in front of him, three stories tall, a glorious sight with its dark green trim and its rows of windows sparkling in the bright summer light.

Alex didn't notice. He was too busy trying to swallow the fear that choked him as he saw the pair of emergency vehicles parked ahead. His gaze swung wide, taking in the carved double doors that led into the house. They were standing wide open.

He slammed the car to a stop, threw open the door and leapt out. Racing across the manicured lawn, he ducked around a Japanese maple, pelted up the shallow brick steps and slid to a halt in the marble-floored foyer. After the glittering warmth of the sunshine, the vast hall felt cool, dusky—

And quiet. Unnaturally, ominously quiet. "Brady! Nicholas! Michael! Hello—is anybody here?"

Silence. For the space of a heartbeat he didn't hear a sound but his own labored breathing. Then he detected a faint tapping noise and a murmur of voices coming from overhead.

He bolted up the wide, curved stairway and along the railed balcony that overlooked the foyer, heading toward the children's wing of the house. Whipping around a corner, he faltered as he approached the boys' oversize bathroom and spied several uniformed men standing inside.

Oh, no. Had Nick been playing sock hockey, slipped and hit his head? Or maybe it was Mikey. Perhaps his youngest son had tried to wash and blow dry the hamster again, only this time had been electrocuted for his troubles instead of merely nipped. Or what if it was Brady? What if, despite all the warnings, Brady had attempted to put another smoke bomb together and—

He drew a deep breath. *Get a grip, Morrison. You aren't going to be worth zip if you keep this up.* Reaching down deep inside, he tapped into the well of icy calm he had discovered when Allison died and shoved aside his panic.

By the time he strode into the bathroom, he had himself frigidly under control. "I'm Alex Morrison. Who's in charge here? What's going on?"

For an instant the room fell silent. The three firemen who were clustered around the wall on Alex's left stopped talking, while a pair of paramedics standing a dozen feet straight ahead turned to stare.

And then the quiet was shattered by a trio of high, young voices. "Daddy!" four-year-old Mikey cried, his face lighting up as he raced around the half wall that separated the bathtub from the rest of the room and launched himself at his father.

"Daddy!" Six-year-old Nick's voice rang with excitement as he pelted after his little brother.

"Daddy?" Brady popped around the corner to stare at his father in undisguised horror. "What are *you* doing here!"

Like Alex himself, all three boys had brown eyes and brown-blond hair. Mikey, slight and angular, had his mother's sweet smile and sensitive nature. Nick was sturdy and round-cheeked, with a sprinkle of freckles across his nose and an easy-to-read expression. But it was Brady who drew the eye. Slim and reedy, with intent brown eyes and an engaging grin, he had more curiosity than a convention of rocket scientists, more energy than a fleet of nuclear submarines and more enthusiasm than a gymnasium of cheerleaders—a combination that attracted trouble the way flowers drew bees.

At the moment, he was staring at his father as if he were an escaped felon caught in a spotlight.

Alex gave the two younger boys a brief awkward hug, then peeled them off his pant legs as he focused on his first-born son. "We wrapped up the negotiations," he said slowly. "I wanted to surprise you."

"But I'm not ready!"

"Ready?" Alex raised one eyebrow. "For what?"

Brady became instantly fascinated with the toe of his sneaker. "Well, you know..." he mumbled. "Stuff."

Alex's apprehension grew. He shifted his gaze to his middle son. "Nicholas? You want to tell me what's going on?"

After a quick sideways glance at his big brother, Nick also developed a sudden infatuation with his feet.

There was a moment's tense silence. And then Mikey tugged on his father's sleeve and said clearly, "Shay's stuck."

Alex's gaze softened as he stared down at his youngest child. "She who's stuck?"

Brady sighed. "Not she, Shay," he murmured.

"It was a mersion of missy, Daddy," Mikey said earnestly. "She saved Bwutus."

Brady sighed again. "Mission of mercy, Mikey."

"Yeah!" Nick chimed. "Everybody knows that. Besides, it was your fault!"

Mikey's lower lip trembled. "Was not."

"Was too! If you'd just holded on to Brutus like you were supposed to, none of this would've happened!"

"*Who* is Brutus?" Alex asked.

Mikey's eyes flooded with tears. "He's my g-gerbil. Uncle J-James sended him for my end-of-school pwesent. Brady gots a lizard and Nick got Ike and Spike. I got Bwutus. He's my bestest fwiend."

Alex's mouth tightened. He made a mental note to call his younger brother James and ask him—again—to refrain from sending the boys any more pets.

Which he'd be sure to do *after* he got to the bottom of the current situation. "So what's Brutus got to do with—"

"Pardon me, fellows," a faint, disembodied voice interrupted. "But do you think you could save the discussion for later and get me out of here? Soon?"

Alex jerked around, telling himself the voice couldn't possibly have come from the floor vent the way he thought it had. "What the—" He stopped in shock as the tallest of the fireman stepped forward, making it possible for Alex to see that the other two men were in the process of lifting the built-in clothes hamper out of the wall. "Is there someone down there?" he exclaimed in disbelief.

"Don't worry, sir." The tall fireman stuck out his hand. "Lieutenant Malloy, Port Sandy Fire Department. The lady—your child-care provider, we gathered from the boys?—says she's fine. As far as we can tell, she only dropped about five feet before the bend in the chute stopped her."

"I . . . see," Alex said, his gaze riveted on the hole on the wall. Truthfully, he didn't see at all. Try as he might, he not only couldn't imagine tall, stately Mrs. Kiltz doing something so undignified, but he also found it hard to believe she'd actually been able to fit in such a narrow space. . . .

"Like I said, don't worry," the lieutenant repeated, nodding at his men to proceed. "We should have her out in no time."

Frozen in disbelief, Alex watched as the firemen fed a line with a noose at the end down the now-gaping hole in his wall. They fished for a moment and then Mrs. Kiltz, sounding very unKiltzlike, called out, "Bingo! Nice toss, guys!"

The firemen grinned and began to reel in the line. Moments later a pair of small, sneaker-shod feet appeared. While one fireman leaned back, keeping the line taut, the other reached forward, grabbed the bare, slender ankles attached to the feet, and pulled.

Like a genie emerging from a bottle, a woman popped out of the depths of the wall. Dressed in khaki shorts and a loose navy T-shirt, her back to the room, she was small and slim, with dark glossy hair and a nice, firm fanny.

Alex had never seen her before in his life.

Shock stole his voice. Before he could recover it, the room erupted in a flurry of activity. First, the paramedics rushed past, blocking the stranger from view as she sank to the ground and they moved in to check her out. Next, all three boys darted over, practically trampling Alex in their haste to get close to the stranger. Everyone began to talk.

"Are you all right, ma'am?" Lieutenant Malloy asked.

"I'm fine," she murmured in a husky alto. "I really appreciate you getting me out."

"Those are pretty nasty scrapes on your legs," one of the paramedics stated. "If you'll just sit still for a minute we can—"

"I'm fine, really," she insisted.

"She's tough," Brady said, a disturbing note of pride in his voice.

"Was it dark?" Nick asked.

"Were you ascared?" Mikey inquired.

"Yes, it was, and no, I wasn't. I had Brutus to keep me company, remember?"

"Hand me a sterile 9-O pack, would you, Bill? I'm sorry, ma'am, but this is going to sting a little."

"Well, Mr. Morrison—" Malloy stepped over to Alex, pulled out a small notepad and began to write in it as he talked "—it looks as if everything turned out all right here. I'll send you a copy of my report, of course, but I might as well tell you right now, I am going to recommend that you close up that chute. In addition to the obvious danger to your children, the thing's a fire hazard." He tore the piece of paper from the pad and handed it to Alex.

It was a citation for violating the county fire code. "Now just one minute—" Alex protested.

Malloy held up a hand for silence as the two-way radio hooked to his belt began to squawk. He listened intently as the dispatcher requested assistance at a house fire with possible injuries and rattled off an address. He unclipped the radio and spoke rapidly into it, before saying to the other men, "Gentlemen, that's only a few miles from here. Let's move it!"

The men went into high gear. The paramedics quickly finished while the three fireman hurriedly repacked equipment, and then all five began an orderly stampede for the door. Not more than fifteen seconds later a pair of sirens began to shrill as the Port Sandy Fire and Rescue Team departed.

Alex tried to staunch a growing sense of disorientation. It's just jet lag, he told himself impatiently. Except that he felt as if he'd entered an entire other dimension rather than merely a different time zone—a feeling that intensified tenfold as he got his first frontal view of the stranger.

Under a short, severely cut mop of inky hair, she had dark, intelligent eyes fringed by sooty lashes, a straight little nose and a surprisingly lush mouth that quirked up at the corners, hinting at a dimple in one cheek. Although she wasn't exactly pretty, her face sparkled with such energy and good humor that it made her extremely compelling. She also had one of the most flawless complexions he'd ever seen.

Like a match being struck, awareness burned a path down his spine and set off a sharp burst of heat inside him.

Would her skin be smooth and creamy...everywhere? Would the generous curve of her mouth feel as good trailing over him as he imagined it would? And what about her eyes? Would they get bigger and darker if he stroked his thumbs across her—

"Hey, Daddy? Aren't you gonna say something?"

Brady's cheerful voice poured over Alex like a bucket of cold water.

What the hell was the matter with him? What did he think he was doing, having carnal thoughts about a woman he didn't even know? In front of his *children*, for God's sake?

All the fear and frustration of the day seemed to coalesce. He felt a sudden surge of anger, at himself, at the situation, at her for undermining his control.

"I don't know who you are," he said abruptly, blanking the emotion from his face and voice with an effort. "But I'm Alex Morrison. This is my house and those—" he nodded at the boys, who were clustered around her as if *she* belonged and *he* was the interloper "—are my sons. And you have exactly ten seconds to tell me who you are, how you came to be in my house and what the heck you were doing in my laundry chute."

She shoved a strand of dark silky hair off her cheek, her gaze never leaving his face. Her mouth quirked up. "Or?"

He couldn't believe her nerve. He glowered at her. "Or else I'll call the police."

Two

Lord love a duck. Beau's big brother was a hunk.

A rude, bad-tempered hunk, but still... Shay stared up at him, feeling as if she'd been poleaxed.

Decked out in spotless white bucks, nubby vanilla-colored linen slacks, a smooth white shirt and a loosely woven, gold-tone tie that matched his eyes, Alex Morrison was not merely gorgeous.

He was perfect.

There wasn't a single strand of his thick, straight, gold-on-bronze hair out of place. Nor was there so much as one, solitary unshaven whisker to mar the splendor of his square chin or lean cheeks. Even his shirtsleeves, rolled back to reveal tan, well-toned forearms, looked as if the folds had been precisely measured exactly to match each other.

He was the epitome of manly elegance. And for some strange reason, the longer she looked at him the more she wanted to wrestle him to the ground and muss him up a little.

For starters, anyway.

Her reaction stunned her. She'd worked with a variety of men over the years and had never before felt an urge to attack one. Frozen with dismay, all she could do was stare when Alex crossed his arms and said brusquely, "Well?" His striking golden eyes bored into her.

Well, what? For the life of her, she couldn't remember the question. "I—I—" *Great. I'm babbling like an idiot.*

Brady, bless his heart, came to her rescue. "Da-a-ad!" the boy wailed, making a strangled sound midway between acute exasperation and utter mortification. "You can't call the police! C-can you?"

The child's distress made Shay forget her own and brought her composure flooding back. "It's all right, sweetie," she murmured, finding her tongue. "I'll handle this." Carefully transferring Brutus to Mikey, she told herself she should actually be glad of this proof that Alex Morrison wasn't as indifferent to his sons' welfare as she'd previously believed.

Even if his behavior was a little heavy-handed.

She took a deep breath, climbed to her feet, squared her shoulders and stuck out her hand. "Hi. I'm Shay Spenser."

Alex's shuttered gaze flicked from her face to her bandaged shins and back again before his fingers closed briefly over hers. He inclined his head a curt inch. "Ms. Spenser." The warmth of his palm was in marked contrast to his icy tone.

He waited. With growing impatience. Until suddenly Shay realized that, despite Mikey's earlier mention of her mission of mercy—and the fact that she'd just *handed* the child his gerbil—Alex expected her to explain herself.

The last of her preoccupation with his looks evaporated.

Well, for heaven's sakes! What did he think? That she'd crawled down the laundry chute to steal his socks and taken Brutus along as an alibi?

She drew herself up to her full height. "Mikey's gerbil got into the hamper. I leaned in to grab him, overbalanced when one of the boys bumped into me, and the latch on the bottom gave way when I fell against it." A trace of asperity crept into her voice. "I believe you know the rest."

"Yes." He made no attempt to disguise his less-than-flattering opinion of it, either. It was apparent in the stiff way he stood, feet apart, hands resting loosely on his hips, his dark gold eyes narrowed at her. "That answers one question. Now, how about the other?"

Piqued by his attitude, she stared right back. "What other?"

"What are you doing in my house? Where's Mrs. Kiltz?"

He was definitely too uptight. Give her a laid-back, just-stepped-out-of-a-wind-tunnel kind of guy any day. "That's two questions."

"Oh, for—"

Brady gallantly took a half step forward and entered the fray. "Mrs. Kiltz quit, Dad."

"What?" Alex's golden gaze jerked toward his oldest son.

"She quit," Brady repeated.

"*When?*"

The boy shrugged, clearly unconcerned with such trifling details. "I dunno.... Day before yesterday, maybe?"

"Actually, it was the day before that," Shay supplied.

"Day before—? Why the he—" catching himself mid-curse, Alex made an admirable attempt to change course "—ck didn't somebody call me?"

Brady frowned sternly at his father. "I did. *You* were supposed to call me back."

Much to Shay's surprise, Alex actually looked sheepish. "You're right. I didn't get the message. But that doesn't explain why—"

"Mrs. Kiltz was nasty," Nick spoke up. "She yelled. A lot."

Mikey nodded solemnly. "Uh-huh. She said we were deviled prawns, Daddy."

At his father's blank look, Brady rolled his eyes. "Devil's spawns, Dad."

At that, Alex went very still and then his mouth tightened ominously.

Aunt Frannie better have her act together, Shay found herself thinking. Because unless she was badly mistaken, come the morning, heads were going to roll in Nannyland.

A little swell of approval washed through her. Maybe Alex wasn't so bad, after all. Maybe he had a headache. Or maybe he was tired. Or maybe his briefs were too tight and that was the cause of his ill humor....

"All right." He laced his hands together and ruined her attempt to give him the benefit of the doubt by turning a speculative, suspicious look on her and the boys that didn't bode well for the future. "So who wants to explain why Mrs. Kiltz said that. And why she quit?" He knit his straight dark eyebrows together—the color startling in contrast to the gilt strands of his hair—and waited.

"Who knows?" Brady said quickly, in a tone that seemed to ask, *Who knew why grown-ups did anything?*

Unfortunately, Mikey took him literally. "I do," the four-year-old said proudly. "It was Ike and Spike, Daddy. Mrs. Kiltz was ascared of them." He turned to his older brothers. "Doncha remember? She screamed really loud when she—ow!" Mikey howled. "Daddy, Brady pinched me!"

Brady rounded his eyes innocently. "I did not!"

Alex's voice rose as he tried to make himself heard over the sudden din. "Who are Ike and Spike?"

"It doesn't matter," Brady said hastily. "What matters is that there was somebody here to take care of us, to make sure nothing bad happened to us. Right?" He stared expectantly at his father.

"Yes, of course, but—"

"Then you should be happy 'cuz Shay was here and she took really good care of us." Brady's mouth pursed for a second as he thought hard, and then his expression cleared. "She made us wash *both* our hands. And eat our vegetables before dessert. And—and she even helped us fix up our fort in the woods."

"Yeah!" Nick joined in enthusiastically. "You should see it now, Daddy! Shay helped us make a trap door. And we cut a hole in the side, so now there's a porthole. Shay knows how to do all kinds of neat stuff."

His pique forgotten, Mikey quickly jumped on his brothers' bandwagon. "She helped us make a flag to fly. It's got skulls and daggers and—"

"Wait." Alex raised his fingers and pinched the bridge of his nose as if to stave off a headache. A second passed before he dropped his hand and regarded the quartet facing him. "I want to be sure I've got this straight. Mrs. Kiltz quit because she was afraid of Ike and Spike, and Aunt Frannie's sent you—" his amber eyes locked on Shay "—to replace her?"

"No—" Shay began.

"No way!" Brady interrupted again. "Shay's cool!"

Alex was starting to look frazzled. "What does being cool have to do with anything?"

"Uncle Beau sent her."

"Beau?"

"I'm staying at his cottage," Shay interjected. "Didn't you get his note?"

Alex shook his head, and she swallowed a groan, which was all the invitation Brady needed to plunge back into the conversation.

"See, Dad, Shay doesn't have a house or a family and stuff. She's all alone. No husband. No little boys of her own." He sent a sharp-eyed look at his father to make sure Alex was paying attention, then gave a heartfelt sigh as if to underscore the sorry state of Shay's life. "And she used to work, but now she doesn't. So Uncle Beau said she could come here for a while and stay at his cottage."

Shay stared at Brady, speechless. Good grief! With just a few well-chosen words, her young friend was making it sound as if she were not only homeless and unemployed, but close to destitute, as well. "Now just a minute—"

"She tells stories," Nick said loudly, getting in his two cents' worth. "About Amazons eating lizards."

Oh. That was better. Now it sounded as if she were merely deranged.

"I'm afraid the boys are giving you the wrong impression," she cut in. "I do tell 'stories' but that's because I'm—"

Alex's voice overrode hers. "You're not from the employment agency?"

"No. I—"

"You're only here because you know my brother?"

She was getting awfully tired of being interrupted. "Not in the Biblical sense," she said firmly. For some obscure reason, it was important she make that clear. "But, yes. We're friends. Colleagues. We work together, you see, and—"

"I'm sorry." He reached up and raked his hand through his hair, and despite her growing frustration, she couldn't help but stare as it fell flawlessly back in place.

How did he do that?

"I misunderstood." His formal, stilted tone wrenched her gaze back to his face. "I thought—well, it doesn't matter what I thought. I owe you my thanks. If you hadn't been here—" He stopped, reached into his pocket, pulled out a money clip, peeled off some bills and then thrust them at her. "Here. For your time and trouble."

Shay looked from him to the money and back again and told herself not to feel insulted. "That's very kind, but no." She stuck her hands in the back pockets of her shorts to underscore her conviction. "Hanging out with your sons has been my pleasure." She glanced fondly at the boys. "They're terrific. I had a great time."

Alex's gaze skimmed over her. His mouth tightened as he made note of her stubborn posture. "I insist. You earned it." Obviously irritated, he glanced away and did a slow, unhurried inventory of the room...throw rugs wadded in a heap in the corner, towels scattered across the counter and the sad remains of the laundry hamper strewn in bits and pieces across the floor. He brought his eyes back to meet Shay's. "I will, of course, take over from here."

"But, Dad!" all three boys protested in unison.

Nick's voice rose above the others. "Shay promised to show us later how to make dinner in a fire pit!"

A small muscle in Alex's jaw twitched. "Not tonight," he said firmly. "I'm sure Ms. Spenser is anxious to get back to the cottage and resume her vacation." His hooded golden gaze swung from his sons' imploring faces to Shay. "You are, of course, welcome to stay *there* as long as you like."

It was a very generous offer—given that the cottage belonged tó his brother. Still, the underlying message was clear. She was not wanted or needed here.

"But, Dad!" Brady repeated. "We want Shay to stay. We like to do stuff with her. We—"

"Hey, Brady, don't worry about it," she said, trying to ease the child's distress. After all, it wasn't his fault his father had all the social grace of a wounded barracuda. "We'll do it another time."

"But—"

"Shh. It's been a *long time* since your dad's been home—" two could play the double message game "—and I'll bet he's anxious to have you all to himself and hear about everything you've been doing." She smiled blandly at Alex; it was clear from the tight set of his jaw that he got her point. "I'll just get my things and be on my way." She took a step toward the door.

"Wait." Alex's command stopped her in her tracks. "Aren't you forgetting something?" He held out the money.

Why, *why*, was he determined to reduce her friendship with the boys to nothing more than a business transaction? She opened her mouth to once more reject his offer, then hesitated as an idea came to her.

After all, there were several excellent local charities that could use a little financial boost. And if she managed to teach Alex Morrison a little lesson about the pitfalls of misdirected noblesse oblige, why, so much the better.

"How much?" she asked slowly.

He blinked. "How much what?"

"How much are you offering?"

Surprise flashed in his eyes at the unexpected turn in the conversation. "Three-fifty."

"Oh." Shay reached out and plucked the bills from his hand. "I'm worth much more than that. Make it five hundred and we'll call it even." She'd match it, she told herself firmly, determined not to give in to a pang of conscience when he did a double take.

To his credit he didn't utter so much as a single word of protest, however. He simply retrieved his money clip, peeled off another crisp hundred and fifty and handed it to her. Yet the flinty look in his eye told Shay she'd made her point.

"Thanks." She pocketed the money.

"Yeah, Daddy," Brady said importantly. "Shay's worth extra 'cuz she won a Howitzer."

She started for the door. "That's *Pulitzer*, Brady."

"Hey, wait up," the boy cried, moving to her side. "I'll help you pack."

"And I could carry your bag if you want." Nick picked up the theme. "I'm real strong."

"Wait for me, wait for me!" Mikey cried, determined not to be left behind. "I wanna help, too!"

A surge of fondness painted a smile on her face. They were really great kids. "Thanks, guys."

She felt Alex's eyes burning a hole in her back all the way to the door.

Incredible. Alex had met some brazen, impudent, nervy women in his day, but Shay Spenser was in a category all by herself.

He recognized her name now, of course. Beau had mentioned her on more than one occasion, usually with a pithy comment when she'd scooped some story he'd been working on.

Alex wondered how she'd talked his brother into letting her come here. But then, beneath his macho exterior, Beau had a notoriously soft heart and a well-known weakness for pretty women. He'd probably taken one look at those big, dark eyes and that exotic mouth and been like putty in her hands.

Still, that was no excuse for allowing her access to Alex's sons. Just as soon as he got the chance, he was going to have to have a talk with his middle brother.

In the meantime Ms. Spenser had better watch her step. Unlike Beau, Alex was neither soft-hearted nor governed by his hormones, despite that odd moment earlier, which he now recognized as nothing more than a temporary side effect of stress.

It wouldn't happen again, and a certain petite brunette would find herself on the receiving end of trouble if she tried to manipulate *him*. She'd gotten away with it once with the money, but he wouldn't be caught out that way again.

Feeling marginally better with that realization, Alex decided he might as well take advantage of the boys' preoccupation with her leave-taking. He headed down the hall to his own suite of rooms, made another quick call to Aunt Frannie's answering machine, stripped out of the clothes he'd had on for too many hours and took a quick shower.

When he opened the bathroom door twenty minutes later, his sons were sprawled on the king-size bed, waiting for him.

He took a long look at their mournful expressions, hitched the towel tighter around his waist and hiked across the pale gray carpet to his dressing area. "You boys get your friend on her way?"

Brady stared up at the skylight in the ceiling and sighed gustily. "Yeah. She looked so sad. Now she's back at the cottage, all alone."

That wasn't entirely true, Alex thought. She had his five hundred dollars for company.

Nick plucked at the down-filled satin comforter. "She said we could come over tomorrow and see her if it was okay with you. Is it okay?"

"We'll see," Alex said, using the universal parent phrase for *no way*. Reaching into a drawer for clean underwear, he watched warily out of the corner of his eye as Mikey slid off the bed, walked over and slipped his sneakered feet into Alex's size-ten dress shoes. The child began to shuffle around, reeling dangerously.

Nick flopped over on his stomach and began to kick his feet up and down. "You know what, Daddy?"

"What?"

"I'm hungry."

Alex gladly welcomed the change of subject. He thought for a second and realized he was, too. Furthermore, it appeared he and the boys were on their own for the evening. "Tell you what. Why don't you go wash your hands and faces while I finish dressing, and I'll take you out to dinner."

Nick scrambled off the bed. "Really?"

For an instant something nagged at him, something he knew he ought to remember, but he couldn't put his finger on what it was. "Really."

Brady popped upright. "Can Shay come?"

"No. This is a family meal."

"Can we go to Letsa Eatsa Pizza?" Nick asked.

Alex sighed. Nick always wanted to go to the pizza joint. Still, it was his first night home. "Sure."

"All right! Come on, Brady." Clearly afraid his father would change his mind, Nick dragged his elder brother off the bed, yanked Mikey out of Alex's shoes and hustled the pair out the door.

Ten minutes later the four of them trooped down the front steps to get in the car. It was then, when Alex saw the open driver's side door and recalled his earlier panicked flight, that his nagging sense of something undone made sense. With a groan, he slid onto the seat and tried the ignition. Sure enough, the battery was dead, drained by the combination of courtesy lights and warning buzzers activated by the open door. *Well, hell.*

Brady shifted restlessly on the seat beside him. "Come on, Daddy. Let's go."

The other two boys bounced up and down on the back seat like a hyperactive chorus line. "Let's go, let's go," they chanted.

With a heartfelt sigh, Alex twisted on the seat to take in all three. "Sorry, boys. The battery's dead. We'll have to do it another time."

First disbelieving, then reproachful, his sons stared at him.

"But you promised," Nick said forcefully.

"That was before I found out the car was dead."

"I'm hungry," Mikey said plaintively.

"I'm not," Nick wailed. "I'm *starved*. What're we gonna do?"

"I know!" Brady said happily. "We can go to Shay's! She can drive us in her car and we can all have dinner together!"

"Yeah!" sang the chorus.

"No," Alex said firmly. He couldn't afford her help. He climbed out of the car. "I'll fix dinner."

The boys climbed out after him, their expressions dubious.

"You can cook?" Brady asked. "Really?"

"Yes. How about toasted cheese sandwiches?"

"Okay," Mikey said.

"Okay," Nick said.

"Yech." Brady made a choking sound and clutched the-atrically at his throat. "I hate toasted cheese." He scowled. "I bet we wouldn't have to eat dumb old toasted cheese if Shay was here. She knows how to cook really good food."

Alex ground his teeth as they trudged back inside. "It'll be fine. You'll see."

It was, too. At first. Even though he wasn't very familiar with the kitchen, since the housekeeper normally did the cooking, Alex easily located the cheese, bread and marga-rine and some potato chips.

He had the cheese sliced and was buttering the bread when the phone rang. Brady answered, spoke for a moment, then looked unhappily over at his father. "It's Ms. Layman from the nanny place."

Alex laid down the knife. "Good." Given his frame of mind, he thought this was one conversation the boys would be better off not hearing. "I'll take it in the study."

"What do you want to talk to her about?" Brady de-manded.

"A new nanny," Alex said firmly. "Hang up after I pick up in the other room."

"But, Dad—"

"I'll be right back." He strode down the hall and into the elegant room he considered his sanctuary. Although the walls and carpeting where done in a restful eggshell color, liberal splashes of navy, gold and maroon made the room unmistakably masculine. He picked up the phone. "Hello? Ms. Layman?"

Francine Layman, an energetic, gregarious woman of sixty, seized the initiative. "Mr. Morrison! I'm so glad you're back! I'm sure you'll be pleased to know that I've convinced Mrs. Kiltz not to sue."

Alex, who'd started to sink down in the big, burgundy leather chair behind the massive, teak desk, shot to his feet. "Excuse me?"

"As long as you'll agree to make a settlement toward her therapy, she's agreed to sign a release absolving you of responsibility."

"Responsibility? For what?"

Frannie uttered a slightly put-upon sigh. "Her breakdown, dear. She still refuses to discuss specifics, simply shudders and whispers about giant, man-eating spiders, but I'm sure that's only temporary. A few sessions with a first-rate therapist, the correct dose of tranquilizers, and she should be right as rain." She paused, then added thoughtfully, "You might consider calling an exterminator, though. Just to be on the safe side."

"Exterminator?" Alex ground out. "*The Terminator* is more like it! The woman walked off and left my children alone and unsupervised! And *you* didn't even bother to contact me!"

"Oh, no, dear. That's not true. I talked to your son, Bradley—"

"Brady."

"Yes, that's right. Such a delightful boy. He assured me he'd spoken to your secretary. He said he was waiting for you to call back and that when you did, he'd have you call me. Oh, dear. Wasn't that true?"

"Yes, but—" Alex began to pace, marching back and forth between the grass-papered walls, which were liberally dappled with evening shadow.

"According to Brady, your fiancée was there and was perfectly happy to take over—"

"My fiancée?" Alex slammed to a stop. "I don't have a fiancée."

There was a tiny moment of silence. "But I called this very phone number, Mr. Morrison. And I spoke with a delightful young woman, a Miss—" there came the faint sound of rustling paper "— Spenser, who assured me she'd be glad to stay with the children until your return. Such a pleasant, charming young woman. After what your son said, I just assumed... Oh, my. Did you two break up, dear?"

Alex clenched his jaw so hard pain shot into his ears. "Ms. Spenser happens to be a friend of my brother's," he said stiffly.

"Oh, my." Frannie sounded unmistakably scandalized. "I've heard of such things, of course, but... how awkward for you."

Puzzled, he did a quick review of the conversation. His spine snapped straight. "Wait a minute! I didn't mean—"

"Please, Mr. Morrison," Frannie interrupted anxiously. "I don't mean to be rude, but I really do think it would be best if we refrain from discussing your personal problems and get back to business."

Alex pinched the bridge of his nose and grimly concluded she was right. Besides, the effort of correcting her mistaken conclusion was probably not worth the added aggravation of prolonging the conversation. "Fine."

"Good." She injected a bright note into her voice. "Is it safe to assume, then, that you'll be wanting a new nanny since you're not getting married?"

He squeezed his eyes shut. "Yes."

"Good, good. How does next week look for you?"

"For what?"

"Why, for conducting interviews."

His hand tightened in a stranglehold around the phone. "How about tomorrow." It was not a question.

"Oh, I don't think—"

"Good. Go with that." With an effort, he kept his tone polite. "I've got work to do. I'm due in New Mexico the end of next week and I need—"

"Daddy?" Mikey stood uncertainly in the doorway.

"Hold on." He covered the mouthpiece and addressed his son. "I'm on the phone, Michael. What do you want?"

"Brady says to ask you if cheese is supposed to turn black."

"It depends. What cheese are we talking about?"

"For the sandwiches."

Alex frowned. "It's turning black? Why?"

"I dunno."

Of course not. "Where is it?"

"With the bread."

He prayed for patience. "Where is the bread?"

"In the toaster."

"Ms. Layman? I have to go. I'll expect to hear from you first thing in the morning. You can tell me then about the candidates you've lined up."

"But—"

He slammed down the phone, scooped Mikey up and rushed down the hall. Between Ms. Spenser, Aunt Frannie, being dog tired and having his wits scared out of him twice in two hours, he'd had about all he could handle. He threw open the kitchen door and plunged inside at the same instant the smoke alarm went crazy.

His gaze shot to the counter. Not only was smoke pouring in an oily stream from the toaster, but the appliance was crackling ominously, as well.

Swearing a silent blue streak, he set Mikey down and leapt across the room, jerked the cord from the outlet and swept the device into the empty sink. Then he stalked over and threw open the outside door to let some fresh air into the smoke-filled room.

He whirled to face the boys. "What the hell do you think you're doing?" he shouted at Brady and Nick, furious as he realized how badly they might have been hurt.

"Uh-oh," Nick said. "You said a bad word."

Brady's jaw rose pugnaciously. "Mikey and Nick were hungry. And you were on the phone forever!"

"I don't care how long I was on the phone! You're lucky you didn't burn the damn house down! Don't you know better than to put cheese in the toaster?"

Nick's lip trembled. "We were only trying to help."

Brady slung a protective arm around his younger brother. "Yeah! How're we supposed to know? It's not like we've got a—a *mom* to show us, you know!"

The boy's logic—plus the wrenching reminder of their lack of a mother—punched a giant hole in Alex's temper.

As swiftly as it had come, the anger drained out of him, replaced by guilt as he registered the mixture of anxiety, misery and defiance on all three young faces. *Way to go, Morrison. You go weeks without seeing your kids, then come home and yell at them.*

Before he could think of what to say, Mikey took a look around at the tableau of angry faces and burst into tears.

Like dominoes falling, the two older boys promptly covered their eyes and also began to sob.

Well, hell. What was he going to do now?

Three

More than slightly out of breath, Shay jogged along one of the wooded paths that crisscrossed the estate. After dropping her things at the cottage, she'd decided to go for a run, hoping the exercise would dispel the jumble of emotions her meeting with Alex Morrison had inspired.

Fat chance. No matter how hard she tried, how fast she ran, or how often she told herself the man was walking proof of the old adage that beauty was only skin-deep, she couldn't get him out of her mind.

Of course, it really had nothing to do with him, she told herself firmly, as she darted around a protruding branch. Her concern was solely for the boys. They were bright, sweet, and funny. In the space of a few weeks they'd managed not just to get under her skin, but also to worm their way into her heart. Mostly because they were three of the most engaging little kids she'd ever met. But also because they were desperate for some adult attention. If there was one thing Shay could identify with, it was that.

Parental indifference had been a fixture of her own childhood, a by-product of being raised by two busy professionals so caught up in their own careers they had no time for their own child. In Shay's case, the experience had ultimately made her independent, self-sufficient and motivated. But it had still been a lonely way to grow up, and it was not the kind of bond she wanted to share with Brady, Mikey and Nick.

They deserved better.

Which brought her back to the problem—all six blond-and-glorious feet of him—and also helped to explain why, she supposed, she couldn't put Alex from her mind.

The situation would sure be easier, she thought crossly, if the man were a tad more approachable. Then she could simply talk to him—diplomatically, of course. Unfortunately it appeared the boys had inherited all of their charm, not to mention their senses of humor, from their mother.

Still, she promised, as she emerged into the clearing in front of the cottage, if the opportunity presented itself, she would try to do something to improve the boys' situation. It was the least she could do, after the way they'd opened their home and their hearts to her these past few weeks.

Slowing to a walk, she wiped her damp face on the tail of her T-shirt, crossed the small patch of lawn and stepped onto the stoop. At first glance the cottage appeared nondescript, a simple, shingled structure with a small stoop and modest carport. Yet its initial appearance was deceiving, since the roof sloped up to meet a back wall made almost entirely of glass that commanded a breathtaking view of Puget Sound.

Inside, the floor plan was open and airy. The kitchen, living and bedroom areas flowed into each other and were filled with creature comforts. The appliances were ultra-modern. The plushly padded chairs and sofas, grouped around the massive stone fireplace, were covered in velvety corduroys and buttery leathers in restful shades of white, turquoise and navy. There was a state-of-the-art stereo CD system and a big-screen TV and VCR. The platform bed that dominated one corner was big but cozy and boasted a feather tick.

However, it was the view that always gave Shay the greatest pleasure. Tonight, evening sunshine glittered like gold dust on the vast expanse of slate blue water that filled the horizon. A large catamaran tacked in the wind, its spanking white sails billowing in a playful breeze. Farther away, purple-gray islands rose out of the haze, their shapes indistinct in the soft golden light.

Sighing with pleasure, she kicked off her shoes and began to strip off her clothes as she made her way toward the bathroom, leaving socks, shorts, shirt and underwear in her wake. She was naked by the time she stepped around the curving glass-block wall onto the tile floor of the oversize shower.

She washed her hair, then turned the shower head to pulse and gave herself up to the sheer bliss of the pounding hot water, the rhythm in perfect sync with the surf outside on the beach.

Except this stretch of Puget Sound didn't have pounding surf, for heaven's sake.

Her head shot up as she realized the steady thumping she heard was actually someone hammering on the front door. She twisted the spigots and scrambled out of the shower. Grabbing a towel, she mopped at her hair, her sense of urgency increasing as the knocking continued. "Hold your horses! I'm coming!" She tossed the towel to the floor, yanked on a clean tank top and a pair of sweat shorts, raked a hand through her hair and dashed for the door.

"What!" she demanded, throwing it open.

"Hey, Shay!" Faces freshly washed and their shirts miraculously tucked into their pants, Brady, Nick and Mikey beamed at her as they stood crowded onto the tiny front porch.

"I bet you're surprised to see us!" Brady cried.

Given the way she and Alex had parted, surprise didn't begin to cover it. "What are you guys doing here?"

"We came to see if you want to drive us to town for some pizza."

"Well, I—"

"Daddy was gonna, but he left his car open and it died," Mikey explained sadly.

"Yeah. And then he said he'd make dinner, but the lady called from the nanny place and the cheese burned and he yelled and we cried and he said a bad word," Nick reported. "He said, 'oh, sh—'"

"That's enough, Nicholas." Alex's cool voice snapped Shay's head around. "You wouldn't happen to have some jumper cables, would you?"

She shook her head, her eyes widening as he stepped out of the deep shadows to her right, where the stoop met the angled support post of the carport. He'd taken a shower, too, she saw. Freshly shaved, he looked like dynamite in a loose black shirt and casually pleated off-black pants. She shivered in reaction, then flushed as she felt goose bumps rise in several strategic locations.

Darn. He was doing *it* again. Making her mind feel dazed, her heart race and her skin feel shivery by simply standing there.

It wasn't until a few seconds later that she realized part of the problem was the breeze. She glanced down, appalled to discover it was molding the soft cotton of her shorts and top to her damp skin—and to those darned goose bumps.

Alex followed her gaze, only to find he'd made a serious mistake at the undeniable evidence that her complexion wasn't her only outstanding attribute. The rest of her was pretty damn...outstanding, also. Lord knew he was getting a firsthand view, because, unless he was badly mistaken, she wasn't wearing a stitch of underclothing.

His whole body went tight at the realization, and a persistent little drumbeat of need kicked to life deep inside him.

Its advent irritated the hell out of him. He didn't need this, not after everything else he'd had to put up with today. What was her problem? Didn't she have sense enough not to come to the door practically naked? Didn't she realize it could be anyone standing there gawking at her?

Yeah. But it's not anyone. It's you, Morrison.

He jerked his gaze away from the ripe swell of her breasts. Locking his gaze on the boys, he tried to remember how the trio had managed to talk him into this in the first place. "I told you this wasn't a good idea. Obviously, we're interrupting. We'll go out to dinner tomorrow night. After the car is fixed." *Without Ms. Spenser.* He stepped off the stoop, expecting them to follow.

Brady didn't budge an inch. "But, Dad! You said you'd ask!"

"Yeah!" Nick agreed. "We already washed our faces again and everything! That's two times in one day."

Mikey stared at his father, his eyes wide and his expression earnest. "You pwomised."

Alex stared back into those eyes so much like Allison's, which were still slightly red-rimmed from crying. *Damn.*

With a resigned sigh he turned back to Shay, careful to keep his gaze on her face. "Look. I can see this isn't a good time for you. But the boys—" he couldn't help the slight stress he put on the word "—were wondering if you could see your way clear to give us a lift into town. I'd be happy to pay for your time and your gas, of course, and—"

"—we want you to have dinner with us!" Brady finished with a rush.

Alex nearly gave himself whiplash as he jerked sideways to stare at his son. "We do?"

"Uh-huh." The boy's expression was guileless. "'Cuz it's the nice thing to do. Isn't it, Daddy?"

Alex decided then and there to add the kid to his growing hit list: Whitset, his brothers, James and Beau, Mrs. Kiltz, Aunt Frannie, Shay and now Brady. Maybe he could get a volume discount. "Yeah. Sure."

Shay made no attempt to disguise her opinion of his sincerity. "Really?" She raised one dark eyebrow skeptically.

All three boys stared expectantly at their father.

"I'd be . . . honored."

Honored, my great-aunt Fanny. Shay had seen men about to face a firing squad look more enthusiastic. Not that he needed to worry. She had better things to do with her evening than spend it with a man who seemed to regard her with the same enthusiasm most people reserved for dental plaque.

Although she did have to admit, a perverse part of her was actually enjoying his discomfort. And there was the chance that an evening spent exposed to his less-than-charming personality might cure her of the fluttery, breathless feeling that overcame her every time she got too close to him. Sort of like aversion therapy.

Because he really *was* great looking. So tall, so broad-shouldered, so lean and lithe and golden. . . .

Then again, maybe it was hopeless. "I'm sorry. I don't think—" She broke off as she felt a tug on her shirt. She glanced down at Brady. "What?"

His big brown eyes were wide with entreaty. "Please? We really, really, really want you to come."

"And I'm so-o-o hungry," Nick said sadly.

Mikey stepped forward and clasped her hand in his smaller one. "Please?"

Aw, heck. She knew she was going to regret this. "Okay. I'd love to."

"All ri-i-ight!" the trio whooped, nearly knocking her down as they swarmed forward to give her a hug.

Forgetting all about Alex, she laughed and hugged them back. "Just let me run a comb through my hair, put on some shoes and grab my keys, okay?" She opened the door wider, stepped back and gestured them in before she turned and headed toward the bathroom. "It'll just take a minute."

"Oh, boy!" Brady grinned happily at Alex, while Mikey and Nick jumped up and down. "Aren't you excited, Daddy? Isn't this great!"

"Oh, yeah," Alex murmured, watching Shay's retreating fanny flex enticingly beneath her clinging shorts. To his disgust, his little drumbeat of need turned into a full-fledged throb. "Great."

He hoped to hell she was going to put on some underwear.

Port Sandy had been founded in 1889. Once an active fishing port, the picturesque little town nestled on Catchup Bay had long since come to depend on tourist dollars for its commerce. Antique and gift shops, bookstores, card shops and ice-cream parlors crowded the half mile of wharves and boardwalks along Main Street. Boats of all sizes and shapes dotted the bay, while graceful Victorian houses painted in a palette of soft pastels perched on the surrounding hills, keeping watch over the colorful scene.

Letsa Eatsa Pizza, tucked away on a side street, was a local, rather than a tourist, hangout. It was small and cave-like, with a dozen booths, half as many tables, a jukebox, a pair of pool tables and a video arcade.

Because of the nice weather, business was light for a Friday night. Alex headed for the largest booth, only to have Brady stop, grab his brothers and literally shove them onto the bench of a smaller one. "We want to sit here," he said, scrambling in after them.

Alex opened his mouth to object, both at the booth's small size and because he and Shay had been left to share a seat, when he caught her look of dismay. For some perverse reason, her reluctance rankled. "After you," he heard himself say, even though he didn't want to sit by her, either.

With a narrow look, she sidled past, giving him ample cause to regret his impulsive words when her breast brushed his arm. A jolt of heat coursed through him. Apparently she'd only managed to secure half the standard ration of undergarments.

She slid gingerly onto the unoccupied seat and moved as close to the far wall as she could.

Alex settled in beside her, careful not to touch her.

Brady beamed at the pair of them, his smile so huge it took up most of his face. "Gee. Isn't this fun?"

"Oh, yeah. Fun," Shay and Alex murmured.

"Can we play video games?" he inquired.

"No." Alex was definitely not in the mood to be left alone with Shay Spenser. Although he wasn't looking at her, he could feel her soft warmth just inches away. And even though he knew, intellectually, that his awareness was the result of being overtired and frustrated in general—by the whole damn day, not just her—it wasn't making his body's lusty response any easier to tolerate. Besides, the boys were the ones who'd wanted her here; they could darn well entertain her.

"But I want to play Space Invaders." Nick said. "Please, Daddy?"

"No."

"Aw, come on," Brady wheedled. "Just a few games?"

"Please, please, please?" Nick begged.

"I don't have any quarters." The minute he said it, he knew it was a mistake. The boys' faces lit up like butane torches.

"I bet Shay has some," Brady said. "She always remembers to bring them, just for us. Doncha, Shay?"

Shay hesitated as four pairs of brown eyes locked on her. Three pairs were shining with total trust; one pair was narrowed warningly. *Great.* "I believe your dad said no."

"But if he did say yes," Brady pressed, practicing early for a career as a prosecuting attorney, "would you have some for us then?"

"Well, yes, but—"

"I knew it!" The eight-year-old whipped his gaze toward his father. "See, Daddy, she does have some! So can we play? Please?"

"Well, since *Shay* has quarters, by all means." Alex sent her a swift look so frigid it could have given frostbite to a polar bear.

Shay's mouth tightened, but she swallowed the retort that sprang to her lips. After all—this was therapy, right? Any moment now her hormones would wake up and realize Alex was more annoying than he was sexy, and the infernal internal hyperventilating that struck her every time he got too close would disappear. Right?

Clinging to that thought, she reached into her purse and pulled out two rolls of quarters, which she quickly divvied up, giving the boys each a few dollars' worth.

"Oooh, thanks!" They slid willy-nilly off the bench and dashed away.

Except for Brady, who stayed long enough to say to his father, "See, Daddy, didn't I tell you? Isn't she wonderful?" He smiled happily and gave Alex a pat on the shoulder. "Now, you guys can have a nice talk. And you don't have to worry about the little kids, because—" he drew himself up "—I'll take care of them for you."

He turned and scampered off. Perplexed by his unexpectedly generous offer—Brady's primary concern was usually *not* his brothers' welfare—Shay glanced sideways at Alex. "What do you suppose that's all about?"

"Beats me." He glanced away as the waitress arrived to take their order. The moment the woman finished, he slid out of the booth and moved to the opposite seat.

Shay heaved a sigh of relief, finally feeling as if she could breathe again. Even so, an awkward silence sprang up that didn't end until after the waitress returned with a basket of bread sticks, a pitcher of root beer and five glasses.

Alex filled a glass and handed it to her. "So, you're a friend of Beau's." It was more a statement than a question,

"Yes, but—"

"Not in the Biblical sense," he finished for her. "So you said. Besides—" he gave her an assessing look "—you're not his type."

She wondered what that meant, then decided she didn't want to know. "Thank goodness. He's not mine, either."

His eyes narrowed at her easy answer, the emotion in those golden depths impossible to read. "How is he, anyway?"

"Fine." She smiled, her affection for Beau obvious. "The last time I saw him he was in top form, making mournful comments about how Italian beer was a far cry from Schlitz."

A faint, answering smile touched the curve of Alex's lips. "Where was this?"

"Trieste. We'd just spent a week in Bosnia, reporting on the fighting there."

"Hmm." He stared into the depths of his glass. "How did you wind up here? This seems like a strange place for a big-time reporter to vacation."

Shay considered her answer, not wanting to lie but not sure she wanted to share her personal business with him, either. "Would you believe I'm doing an exposé on household help?"

His expression hardened. "No. How about the truth?"

Determined to keep things light, she gave a gusty sigh. "I was afraid you'd say that." She picked up a bread stick. "Actually, I'm considering a career change, and your brother was nice enough to offer his place while I hash things out." Of course, she hadn't phrased it quite that way when she'd spoken to Alex's brother.

What she'd said to Beau was, "I'm going to quit."

To which Beau had replied, "Why the hell would you want to do that?" Slightly taller than his brother, with medium brown hair and whiskey-colored eyes, he'd rubbed a hand over a whisker-rough cheek and stared at her in patent disbelief.

She'd shrugged. "It's just . . . not any fun anymore." As an explanation, it had sounded lame even to her own ears.

"This is about us getting shot at on the way back to the checkpoint, isn't it? Damn! I knew we should've taken the other road. If I'd just—"

"This isn't about you, Morrison," she'd said before he could get too wound up. "It's about me. I've been thinking about it for a long time. Sure, the risk is part of it, but it's not all of it." How could she explain that with every passing day, the job that had once meant everything to her was no longer enough?

It seemed she didn't have to. "It's just a job, Spenser," he'd said shrewdly. "It's not supposed to be a holy mission."

Her mouth had quirked. "Right. I suppose you're going to claim you take the risks you do for the fabulous money and the wonderful perks?" She'd glanced pointedly around the café's dingy interior. "Don't insult us both. You do what you do because you're insatiably curious, because you love knowing what's really going on and because you feel an obligation to make sure everyone else knows it, too. And I used to feel the same way. Only lately . . . I don't know. I seem to have lost my edge." That was one way to describe the increasing sense of emptiness, the inexplicable restlessness, the indefinable longing for something more that had been growing steadily in her over the past year.

He'd sat back and regarded her thoughtfully. "How long's it been since you had a vacation?"

"I don't know. A while. Does it matter?"

"Hell, yes." He'd drummed his fingers on the table. "You can't quit. Next to me you're the best damn journalist I know." He'd pursed his lips and thought for a moment. "You like kids?" he asked finally.

She'd narrowed her eyes at him. "If you're about to spout some macho baloney about this having to do with my biological time clock, I'd advise you to forget it."

He'd clapped a hand to his heart and assumed a wounded expression. "God, Spenser, you're suspicious. I'd never say such a thing." A spark of mischief had lit his eyes. "Although, if you *were* pining for a chance to become a mother, I suppose I could be persuaded to sacrifice my virtue to the cause."

"Some virtue. You've conquered more European territory than Napoleon and Hitler combined."

He'd grinned. "Jealous?"

"Don't you wish."

He'd winked. "Maybe I do at that. But the reason I *asked*—" he'd retrieved a ring of keys from his pocket, slid one off and pushed it across the table at her "—is because of this. It's to the place *I* call home, a cottage I keep at my brother's place north of Seattle. If you're looking for somewhere to kick back and do nothing, it's perfect. The catch is, you have to put up with my nephews. Now, don't get me wrong, they're great little guys, but they can be a trifle... overwhelming."

She'd stared at the key, caught off guard both by the unexpectedness of the gesture and by the sudden intensity of her longing to stay in a real home for a change. Then her better sense had kicked in. "What about your brother and his wife? I can't just barge in on a pair of total strangers."

"Don't worry about it. Alex bought the place after his wife, Allison, died. I'll drop him a line to let him know you're coming, but he'll probably be so busy working he won't even know you're there. Heck, you probably won't be there very long, anyway. Either the boys will drive you nuts, or you'll be so bored you'll be clamoring to come back to work."

Shay had doubted that. She'd reached a crossroads in her life and she knew it. Still, the chance to stay somewhere other than a hotel or a boarding house while she figured out her future had been too tempting to resist. "Well, okay. But only if you'll let me pay some rent."

"No way," he'd said firmly.

Sitting in Letsa Eatsa Pizza a month and a half later, Shay grinned as she recalled the argument that had ensued.

Her smile faded, however, as she also remembered how she'd looked across the table at Beau's good-looking face that day and wondered why there'd never been a single spark of attraction between them.

Well, now she knew.

She'd been waiting to meet his rude, stuffed shirt of a big brother so *he* could light her fire.

As if he'd read her mind, Alex sat back and stretched, managing to look incredibly elegant and sexy at the same. He also looked decidedly skeptical. "You're really thinking of changing careers?"

"Yes." Clearly, he didn't believe her. "Why shouldn't I?"

"Why quit when you're on top?" he countered. "You did win a Pulitzer."

And it had been right after that when everything had started to change, although Shay was still trying to figure out why. She shrugged. "I want to try something different."

"Like what?"

"I haven't decided." She was certainly discovering that she preferred asking questions to answering them, however. "Maybe I'll go into baby-sitting. I hear the money's pretty good."

He sent her a dour look. "Very funny."

"What about you? Did your deal go through?"

He took a swift swallow of root beer, nodding as he set his glass down. "Yes, and not a moment too soon. I'm supposed to be in the Southwest next week and it was starting to look as if I wasn't going to make it."

"Oh." She tried to sound neutral, but her dismay must have shown.

His expression tightened. "You have a problem with that?"

"No, of course not," she said hastily. "It's only... you just got home."

A muscle ticked to life in his jaw but his voice remained even. "That's right. And I'm leaving again next week. I have to make a living like everyone else."

"But—"

"Look, I'm sure you mean well," he said impatiently. "And I really appreciate what you did, taking over the past few days. It's clear the boys like you. But I don't need anyone telling me how to raise my sons. I'm quite capable of making sure they have everything they need."

"Except your time," she murmured.

The chiseled line of his mouth flattened out. "Pardon me?"

"Nothing," she said hastily, appalled at her own presumption. *So much for diplomacy.* What was it about him, she wondered a little wildly, that hit her hot button and made her act so recklessly? "I just—" *What?* Had decided on the basis of a five-week acquaintance that he was raising his children all wrong? Wished he would lighten up? Wondered what it would take to make him really smile?

Thankfully, before she could dig herself in deeper, the boys' raised voices claimed their attention.

"It's my turn, Nick!"

"Is not! I get to play another game, Brady."

Alex climbed to his feet. "Excuse me." His voice was clipped. "I'd better go take care of this."

"Of course." He was gone before she finished speaking. Uncertain what to expect—harsh words, a show of force—she twisted around to watch him stride toward the game nook, ready to leap up and defend the boys if they needed it.

Instead, he settled the dispute between Nick and Brady with a few firm words and a flip of a quarter. Then he bent down to listen to something Mikey had to say, only to nod, straighten and disappear around the far partition. He reappeared a few seconds later with a sturdy rubber footstool, which he placed before a Tiny Toons game.

Shay had to admit she was puzzled by his unexpected performance. He wasn't behaving the way she expected an indifferent, absentee father to act. Her confusion grew as he went to lift Mikey onto the stool, and the little boy gave him a quick, spontaneous hug for his troubles. Alex froze—there was simply no other way to describe it—before depositing the boy on the stool and stepping quickly away.

Well, good grief. What was that all about?

She had no time to decide since the waitress chose that moment to come bustling up. "One pepperoni with extra cheese and one house special," the woman said cheerfully, sliding the large round trays onto the table.

She had barely enough time to step out of harm's way as, with shouts of "Oh, boy!" and "It's about time!", the boys came galloping over, generally behaving as if it had been months instead of hours since they'd eaten last. Chaos ensued, and it was some time before things settled down enough to carry on any sort of conversation.

"Are you having a good time?" Brady finally asked Shay after he'd wolfed down four pieces of pizza without coming up for air.

"Of course I am." Grateful that he and his brothers hadn't caught the tension between her and their father, she smiled at the youngster who was sitting beside her.

He smiled back. "That's good." He looked over at Alex. "How about you?"

"Sure," Alex said brusquely.

Brady turned back to Shay. "Uncle James says Daddy's a good catch, you know. He says he's got a big car and a big house and a big—"

"Brady!" Alex's sharp voice cut the boy off. "That's enough."

"Gee, Dad, I didn't say anything wrong, did I?" Brady stared questioningly at his father.

"It's not polite to repeat what other people have told you," Alex informed him, avoiding Shay's amused gaze. He signaled for the check.

"Oh." The eight-year-old thought about that. "You mean I shouldn't say how Uncle Beau said you were so grumpy because you never got any—"

"Brady." Alex's tone was lethal.

Brady, however, was completely unfazed. "—time off?" he finished innocently.

Shay bent her head and coughed to cover a gurgle of laughter, the boy's performance and Alex's reaction restoring her good humor. Before Brady could get in another lick, however, the waitress trotted over with a box for their left-over pizza and the bill.

She reached for it without thinking.

So did Alex.

Their fingertips bumped. His palm slid across the V of her thumb to enfold the back of her hand. They looked at each other.

Shay suddenly felt hot.

It's nothing, she told herself firmly. She was probably coming down with something. A cold. The flu. *Terminal lust.*

Alex indicated the bill with a curt nod of his head. "I'll get that."

She snatched her hand away and somehow managed to dredge up what she hoped was a nonchalant smile. "Hey—anything you want."

For a split second she would've sworn something dangerous flickered in the depths of his beautiful eyes. And then Nick knocked the half-full pitcher of icy root beer into his dad's lap and Alex leapt to his feet with a yowl of surprise.

Needless to say, *that* was the end of *that.*

Four

"That sure was funny," Brady said, chuckling as Alex tucked him into bed. "You shot up just like a rocket!"

"I'm glad you found it so entertaining," Alex said tiredly.

All he wanted to do was go to bed. The house was locked, Mikey and Nick were already safely tucked in. The only thing between Alex and sleep was Brady who, unfortunately, seemed wide awake and ready for a lengthy chat.

"You know what I was wondering, Daddy?"

"No. What?"

"I was wondering...do you think cats have belly buttons?"

Alex straightened and just stared at his son.

"Well? Do they?"

He realized he didn't have a clue what went on in the kid's mind. Furthermore, the wisest thing he could do would be to answer noncommittally and beat a hasty path to the door. Yet, as bushed as he was, he felt a prickle of suspicion he was afraid to ignore.

After they'd arrived home and he'd changed clothes, he'd been given a tour of the family menagerie. Somehow, in the weeks he'd been gone, the ranks had grown from two silky mice, one hamster, a parakeet and five goldfish to include Brutus the gerbil, a lizard, a garter snake, an injured bat the boys claimed to be nursing back to health and—he shuddered—the infamous Ike and Spike, who happened to be a pair of tarantulas, thus explaining Mrs. Kiltz's breakdown.

He did not, however, remember a cat.

"Why do you want to know?" he asked cautiously. "We don't have one, do we?"

Brady grinned and shook his head. "Naw. I just wondered."

Relieved, Alex began to pick up the dirty clothes dropped on the floor.

"Daddy?"

"Hmm?" One more question and he was out of here, he thought, edging toward the door.

"Did you love Mommy?"

He stopped in his tracks, the abrupt change of subject catching him off guard. "What?"

"Did you love Mommy?"

"Yes. Very much," he said quietly.

"Did you think she was pretty?"

"I thought she was beautiful," he said, remembering.

He'd met Allison at college. Blond and blue-eyed, with a soft voice and a kind heart, she'd been as delicate as a fairy queen. He'd fallen in love with her the first time he'd laid eyes on her.

"Did you like being married?"

"Yes." He leaned over and picked up a single bright red sock. He looked around but the mate was nowhere to be found.

"I bet that means you'd like to get married again, wouldn't you?"

"Maybe." But not likely. Alex would never forget how he'd felt after Allison died, as if someone had shoved a hand down his throat and ripped out his heart. Nor would he forget how helpless he'd been in the face of his small sons' fear and sadness and confusion. He didn't intend to ever be that vulnerable again. "It's not that easy, Brady," he hedged. "I'd have to meet just the right lady and she'd have to be very special."

The boy mulled that over for a moment. "Shay's special," he said eventually. "She's pretty, too. Don't you think so?"

This change of subject was just as disconcerting as the last. Out of the blue, Alex suddenly remembered that moment at the end of dinner when he'd held Shay's hand in his. He recalled the softness of her skin, the fragile bones beneath it, the delicacy of her fingers compared to his. He remembered, too, the way the pulse in the base of her throat had begun to throb and how she'd moistened her peach-tinted lips with her tongue as they'd stared at each other. A flush had bloomed across the rising curve of her cheeks.

He'd felt an answering rush of heat somewhere lower.

"Well?" Brady said persistently. "Don't you think she's pretty?"

"Sure." She was pretty damn annoying—and he didn't want to talk about her. "It's time to go to sleep," he said firmly.

"But I'm not tired."

"Well, I am."

"Okay, but—just answer one more question. You aren't going to go away again for a while, are you?"

Alex sighed. "I'm afraid so, Brady."

The boy bolted upright. "But you can't! I mean—who's going to take care of us?"

"Ms. Layman's going to send some ladies out to interview tomorrow."

"But we don't want another dumb old nanny! They're yucky! What we need is a mo—"

"Look," Alex interrupted, holding on to his patience by a thread. "Don't worry about it, okay? We'll talk about it in the morning."

The boy flopped back on the bed. "You promise?"

"I promise."

His expression leveled out. "Okay." He regarded his father intently. "Daddy?"

"What?"

"Don't worry about not knowing about the cats. I'll ask Shay. She'll know. She knows everything."

Alex sighed. He should've seen it coming. It was the perfect end to the perfect night. "Right." He headed toward the door.

"Daddy?"

He turned around. "What is it *now?*"

"I'm glad you're home. I missed you." The boy smiled, a lopsided grin sweet enough to melt a stone, then burrowed under the covers and closed his eyes.

Alex's heart clenched.

But all he said as he switched off the light was, "I missed you, too, son. Good night."

Brady waited until he heard his father's footsteps fade away. Then he got out of bed, tiptoed over and shut the door. Making his way unerringly across the moonlit room, he padded to his desk and turned on the small clip light there.

He picked up his little tape recorder and switched it on.

"Testing, testing," he whispered. "This is micromini cassette number two."

He cleared his throat, thought for a minute, then spoke.

Hey, Uncle Beau, it's me, again...Brady. I just want to let you know that Daddy finally came home and met Shay, and everything is cool, even though stuff didn't go quite the way I planned.

That's 'cuz Daddy didn't call like he was supposed to, and Shay fell down the laundry chute and the firemen came and Daddy was sort of cranky. But after I told him how cool Shay is, he was so happy he gave her five hundred whole dollars for taking such good care of us! Not only that, but he and Shay and the guys and me went on our first date tonight. Daddy and Shay sat together and Daddy says he thinks Shay's pretty. The only problem is, he has to go on another dumb old business trip, so he thinks he has to get us a *new* nanny.

I don't want you to worry about it, though, 'cuz I've been thinking about it and I've got a plan. All I've gotta do is make sure nobody else wants the job and Daddy will ask Shay to do it and he'll get to see she's perfect for us. Simple, huh? I mean—what could go wrong? So for now, this is me, Brady Morrison, your favorite nephew, signing off.

Oh—except for P.S. I'm sending you nine whole dollars and forty-two cents. Can you buy a big diamond ring? And send it as soon as you can? Thanks.

With a nod of satisfaction, Brady clicked off the recorder.

He rewound the little tape, then ejected it and dropped it in one of the already-stamped, preaddressed padded envelopes he'd asked Shay to get for him. He added the money, then licked the envelope and propped it up so he'd be sure to remember to mail it in the morning. Then he switched off the light and crawled into bed.

Yep. Once he'd taken care of the nanny problem, he could concentrate full-time on Operation Mommy.

Smiling with anticipation, he fell fast asleep.

"I still don't see why we have to have a dumb old nanny," Brady said peevishly the next morning for what had to be the fifteenth time.

He and his brothers were seated on the couch in the living room, which had white brocade chairs and sofas, mahogany tables, enough potted palms to decorate a mortuary and an oriental rug the size of a football field.

With a little help from their father, all three boys had dressed in matching white T-shirts tucked into navy shorts. Their hair was slicked back, their hands and faces washed. Their legs, too short to reach the floor, stuck straight out.

"Because." Alex glanced at his wristwatch and frowned. It was already ten-thirty, which meant the first potential replacement for Mrs. Kiltz was fifteen minutes late. "You need someone to take care of you."

The day had started to go sour the moment he'd awakened, and it wasn't getting any better. After a restless night filled with wild dreams of getting to know a certain prize-winning reporter— in the Biblical sense—he'd finally fallen into a sound sleep at dawn. The next time he'd looked at the clock, it had been after nine. Needless to say, he'd overslept.

He'd rushed downstairs to find the boys were not just awake, but up and in the process of destroying the kitchen. Mikey, it seemed, had invited Brutus to breakfast, only to have the troublesome gerbil escape. In the course of a heated but unsuccessful chase, the boys had managed to knock a canister of flour off the counter, topple the spice rack and spill a pitcher of apple juice onto the floor.

Alex had just started to clean up when Mrs. Lent, the housekeeping temp, had wandered in. She'd taken one look at the mess, said she had a headache and announced she was going home.

About the only good thing that had happened was that Aunt Frannie had managed to line up four candidates for him to interview. One of them, she'd assured him cheerfully, was bound to be just what he was looking for.

Unless Aunt Frannie was sending someone who came with her own whip and chair, Alex wasn't quite so optimistic.

"Why can't you take care of us?" Nick demanded.

"Because. I have to work."

"Why can't Shay take care of us?" Brady asked.

"Because. That's not her job."

"But she likes us!"

"I'm sure she does. But you're forgetting she's only going to be here for a little while."

"But we want her to stay longer," Brady said stubbornly.

"And we don't want any dumb old nanny," Nick asserted.

"Too bad, because you have to have one." Alex struggled against a pang of guilt at the unhappiness he could hear in both boys' voices. "Look, we'll find just the right person, I promise." He walked to the window as he heard a car drive up.

"But we already di—" Nick began, only to break off when Brady kicked him in the shin.

Oblivious to the byplay, Alex turned and headed for the front door. "Okay, here we go." At Brady's petulant look, he added, "Trust me. Everything will work out."

Brady exchanged a long look with his brothers. Then he settled back against the couch and folded his arms across his chest. "Oh, yeah?" he murmured. "We'll see about that."

Due to the boys' talent for blowing through nannies as if they were tissue paper, Alex had the process of interviewing prospects down to a science. First he would sketch out what he expected, give an overview of everyday duties, then outline pay and benefits. Next he would ask key questions on subjects such as handling disputes and giving affection, then answer any queries the interviewee might have.

The first candidate was Ms. Jernigan. Barely out of her teens, she had fuzzy brown hair, enormous blue eyes, a build like a Number Two pencil and a timorous manner.

Long before the interview reached the question-and-answer segment, Alex had concluded she was too inexperienced to handle the boys. He was just starting to wrap things up, when, out of the corner of his eye, he saw Brady reach around Nick and nudge Mikey with his toe.

A moment later, Mikey slipped off the couch, came over and tugged on Alex's sleeve. "Daddy?"

"What is it, Michael?"

The child crooked his finger, motioning his father closer so he could whisper in his ear. "I gotta go."

Alex straightened. "Now?"

The four-year-old nodded solemnly.

"Do you need help?"

The boy shook his head adamantly.

"All right, then," Alex said. "Go on."

Mikey raced off, and Alex turned back to Ms. Jernigan. "I believe you were telling me about your philosophy on discipline?" he said politely.

"Oh, yes. I believe if you share your concerns with a child about the possible disruptive potential of his or her negative behavior—"

"Daddy?"

"You're interrupting Ms. Jernigan, Brady."

"I'm sorry. But I'm worried about Mikey."

Alex turned to stare at his eldest son. "You are?"

"Uh-huh." The boy turned solemnly to Ms. Jernigan. "See, he's just a little kid and sometimes he does stuff he's not supposed to. I'm the oldest, so I try to keep an eye on him. I think I better go see if he's okay."

His ardent delivery—and that recently observed nudge—set off Alex's warning system. "Tell you what," he said, determined to nip any attempted shenanigans in the bud. "You stay here and I'll go check on your brother."

Brady stiffened. "But, Dad—"

"I said, I'll go." Alex came to his feet, feeling a grim little ping of satisfaction at Brady's crestfallen look. "You visit with Ms. Jernigan." He gave the boy a meaningful glance. "Be nice. I'll be right back."

Brady looked sad but resigned. "Yes, Daddy."

Alex checked all four downstairs bathrooms before he located Mikey in the last one. The child was standing in front of the mirror, staring sadly at his reflection.

"Michael? What are you doing?"

The boy flushed. "Nothing," he said quickly.

Too quickly. Alex studied the child's reflection, frowning as he realized one side of Mikey's head looked misshapen. He came further into the bathroom and gently but firmly turned the child to face him, relaxing when he saw the cause of the problem. One side of Mikey's hair was plastered to his skull with what had to be an entire tube of hair gel. "That's an interesting hairstyle," he said neutrally.

"I just wanted to try some," Mikey said tremulously. "And now the comb's stuck, Daddy."

Sure enough, when Mikey turned a little more, Alex could see there was a comb mired in a blob of gel behind the boy's ear.

Alex sighed. "It's all right." He snagged a towel off the rack and boosted Mikey up onto the counter. "A little water and you'll be as good as new."

True to his word, Alex soon had Mikey looking like his old self. Not long after that they rejoined the others.

The second they walked in, Ms. Jernigan swiveled anxiously around to stare at them. "Is—is everything all right?"

Alex was taken aback by her show of concern. "Sure. We had a slight problem, but we threw a little water on it and that took care of it, didn't it, Michael?"

"Uh-huh." The little boy nodded.

Nick and Brady made odd choking sounds as Ms. Jernigan said faintly, "You—you had to throw water on something?"

Alex frowned at her obvious distress. "It was nothing. Mike here tried a little experiment with his hair and—"

"His hair! Oh, dear!" She leapt to her feet and began to beat a slow but steady retreat toward the foyer. "I'm so sorry, Mr. Morrison, but I—I'm sure I'm not the right nanny for you. I—I only went to nanny school for two months. I'm simply not equipped to deal with a . . . a special needs child. Especially not a destructive one. I mean—" she sent Mikey a wary look "—your little boy looks very sweet, and I'm sure he's simply going through a stage, but well—I don't even like candles on my birthday cake!"

Alex stared at her in astonishment. "What the blazes are you talking about?"

An unfortunate choice of words. Ms. Jernigan gave a little moan, clutched her high-necked dress to her throat and scurried closer to the door. "There's no need to pretend. The boys told me about Michael's . . . problem. How the firemen had to be called yesterday, about how the kitchen caught on fire later . . ."

"They did, huh?" Alex's gaze shot from the young woman's stricken face to Brady and Nick, who were staring fixedly at their feet.

"Yes! And I'm so sorry for your trouble, but I'm afraid you'll have to find someone else to help you!" With that, she spun and fled.

Alex stood rooted to the spot and slowly counted to ten.

Eight times.

He turned. His gaze bore into the older boys. His voice was icy calm. "All right. Does one of you want to tell me what you said to make that lady think your brother is a pyromaniac?"

Brady and Nick exchanged a look, then glanced at Alex and shook their heads. "Nope," they said in unison.

The doorbell rang.

Brady jumped to his feet. "Gee, Dad." Careful to give Alex a wide berth, he scooted toward the door, Nick hot on his trail. "That must be our next appointment."

Ms. Kay turned out to be a practical, talkative lady in her fifties. She had glasses, wore her hair in a bun and smelled faintly of vanilla and cinnamon. She had raised two lovely daughters, she explained to Alex, and had decided to become a nanny because she missed the joys of child rearing.

At the moment, joy was not the word that came to Alex's mind in reference to his kids, but he refrained from saying so. After all, unlike Ms. Jernigan, Ms. Kay had some experience. Surely she knew that little boys could occasionally be a handful.

It turned out she did. And by the time they reached the end of the interview, Alex had decided Ms. Kay would do just fine. Feeling magnanimous with victory in sight, he turned to the boys. "Do you have any questions?"

There was a moment's silence, then Brady said, "Do you like pets, Ms. Kay?"

Alex felt a stirring of approval. It was a question he should have asked.

"Oh, yes!" Ms. Kay said warmly. "In fact, I have a lovely canary. His name is Skookums."

The boys exchanged another one of those looks Alex couldn't interpret. Remembering the suspicious nature of Mrs. Kiltz's breakdown—among other things—he said hastily, "I think I ought to warn you, some of my sons' pets are a trifle exotic."

Ms. Kay beamed at him. "Oh, how exciting. My Lisa once had an Angora rabbit. And my Skookums is an exceptional singer. Why only last week he—"

The phone rang. Alex waited a second, then remembered he didn't have a housekeeper to answer it. "Excuse me," he said, interrupting. He promised himself he'd set Ms. Kay straight on the exact nature of the boys' menagerie when he got back. He sent them a warning look. "No story telling," he ordered as he stood and started out of the room.

"Yes, Daddy," they said sweetly, in chorus, as Ms. Kay continued to wax poetic about Skookums's impressive singing abilities. Judging she had things under control, Alex stepped across the foyer into his study.

He picked up the receiver. "Hello?"

"Mr. Morrison? This is Arnie, from Arnie's We-Come-2-U Automotive. I'm returning your call about your car—"

A bloodcurdling scream rent the air.

"Arnie? Could you call back?" He slammed down the phone and bolted into the hall in time to see Ms. Kay race across the foyer toward the door, flapping her hands wildly as if to hold off a hoard of invisible attackers. The boys were right behind her.

"What the devil's going on?" he roared.

Ms. Kay wrenched at the doorknob, her glasses askew, her hairdo in shreds. Trembling violently, she stared accusingly at Alex. "Ms. Layman said you'd had a slight problem with pests, but I never imagined...it just never occurred to me—" Another enormous shudder racked her. "I'd never sleep a wink, thinking one of those creatures might swoop down and attack me in my sleep."

"But what—"

"No! I simply can't! I'm sorry!" She yanked open the door and fled down the stairs without further explanation.

Stunned, Alex strode outside to watch as she leapt into her car and sped off. He turned to confront the boys, who had followed him outside. "All right. *What happened?*"

Brady shrugged nonchalantly. "I dunno. We were talking about pets. She told us all about Skookums—" he rolled his eyes "—which, if you ask me, is a really stoopid name—"

"Brady," Alex said warningly.

The boy sighed. "Okay, okay. Well, see, she asked if I had a favorite pet and that's when I remembered Belly was asleep in my pocket. So I took him out to show her and she just went... wacko." He shook his head. "Poor Belly. It wasn't *his* fault. He tried to get away and sort of got tangled in her hair."

"Belly? Who's that?"

"You know, Belly LaGoosey. Remember, I told you last night, how Shay found him and named him for that old actor guy. The one who goes—" the youngster bared his incisors ghoulishly and intoned in a truly terrible Transylvanian accent "—'I vant to drink your blood.' Remember?"

Alex couldn't believe it. Shay again, disrupting his life, and she wasn't even here! He should have known. He should have— "Wait a minute. Are you talking about Bela Lugosi?"

"Yeah. That's what I said."

"Belly's the *bat?*"

"He's sure not some dumb old canary."

Alex's jaw worked furiously, but he couldn't think of one word he wanted to say that was suitable for the boys to hear.

Misinterpreting his father's silence, Nick stepped over, reached up and gave Alex a reassuring pat on the back. "It's okay, Daddy. Don't worry. Belly didn't get hurt."

"Yeah," Mikey said. "His wadar was alweady jammed."

Ms. Marks had a mane of fire-engine red hair that stuck straight up like Woody Woodpecker's and a mouth full of neon-banded braces. Once you got past that—and her lime green catsuit and thigh-high boots—she seemed quite personable, although Alex had to admit he wasn't wild about pierced eyebrows. And he did wonder about her suitability as a role model when she accepted the cup of coffee he handed her and he saw the snake tattoo twined around her wrist. Between the reptile's forked tongue was the inscription, Killer Forever.

Nick saw it, too. "Cool," the boy said avidly. Once more back on the couch with his brothers, he slid forward to get a better view.

Ms. Marks preened and held out her arm. "Killer's my old man. We're going to get hitched." She frowned. "Just as soon as he's out of jail."

Brady looked suitably impressed. "He's in the slammer? Really?"

Ms. Marks snapped her gum, seemingly unconcerned that it might stick to her dental work. "Uh-huh. He's doing two to five, but we figure he'll be out in September for good behavior."

"Did he kill somebody?" Nick asked hopefully.

Ms. Marks giggled. "No, silly. Killer's real smart. What he did, see, was figure out a way to tap into the home shopping network on his computer and order stuff without paying." She raised her coffee cup to her lips and sighed dreamily. "Killer's not just a plain old hacker. He's a computer *artiste.*"

Brady's eyes lit up. "Wow! Do you think you could show me— "

Alex stood up abruptly, leaned over and snatched the coffee cup from her hand. "Thank you, Ms. Marks." He slid a hand under her elbow, assisted her to her feet and began to propel her toward the foyer. "It's been...educational. You might mention to Aunt Frannie I'll be in touch." *She can bank on it.*

"Well, gee," Ms. Marks said truculently. "You don't have to get your buns in a sling, mister. Besides—" she stabbed a fingernail toward the upstairs bannister, nearly taking out a chunk of Alex's ear "—I wouldn't work here, anyway. You've got rats." With a sniff, she yanked open the door and waltzed out.

Alex's gaze shot to where she'd pointed, and sure enough, there was Brutus, scampering happily along the upper rail like a furry tightrope walker.

Alex knew how low he'd sunk when he realized he was actually glad to see the little creature.

Three down, one to go.

Alex breathed a sigh of relief as a sedate blue sedan stopped in the drive and an older lady with short white hair, perfect posture and a no-nonsense air climbed out. According to Aunt Frannie, the background check on Ms. Brunhilde Kneivel hadn't come back yet, but she'd received perfect scores at nanny school.

Alex was pleasantly surprised to find that while brusque, Ms. Kneivel didn't seem unkind, although she did have a disconcerting habit of stressing certain words as if they were in capitals.

"Do you like pets?" he asked after they'd gone through the more formal routine.

"Of course. Animals are our Friends."

"We're not talking your usual dogs and cats here," he said bluntly, too tired to beat around the bush. "The boys have a bat. And a lizard, some tarantulas and a variety of rodents."

Ms. Kneivel nodded with approval. "Good. As a child, I myself had a boa constrictor. Taking care of pets teaches Responsibility." She smiled blandly at Alex's sons. "Boys should have Lots of Responsibility."

"Good point." Alex steepled his fingers. "How do you feel about vivid imaginations? Tall tales?"

"Not to worry. I can tell like that—" she snapped her fingers loudly "—when I am not being told The Truth. With me, your sons will soon learn that Honesty is the Best Policy."

The boys stared at her mournfully. From their expressions it seemed clear they knew they'd met their match.

Alex, who was suddenly feeling pretty good, took pity on them. "Why don't you guys go ahead and run upstairs. Change into your swimsuits and I'll take you for a swim after Ms. Kneivel and I go over a few details."

"'Kay," they said glumly.

Alex watched them trudge to the door, then turned to Ms. Kneivel. "If you're interested, the job is yours. I'd want a two-week trial period, of course, which I'm sure Ms. Layman already explained, but—" The phone trilled.

He sighed. "Excuse me. Just let me get that and—"

Ms. Kneivel inclined her head. "Please. Go ahead."

"You are interested, then?"

She looked admiringly around the big room. "Oh, yes."

With that settled, Alex went to his study. It was Arnie again. This time they were able to talk without interruption. Alex explained the problem and arranged for a service call.

By the time he hung up, he felt great. Everything seemed to be falling into place.

He was a little surprised, therefore, when he stepped into the hall and found Ms. Kneivel waiting for him.

"When would you like me to start?" she asked briskly. Her purse, a large vinyl affair, was open a crack. She rooted around inside it, apparently searching for her car keys.

"Is tomorrow too soon?"

"No, no, that would be fine—"

"Hey, Ms. Kneivel!" Nick called. Alex looked up to see the boys come racing along the upstairs hallway. "You want to see my ant farm?" Flanked by his brothers, the six-year-old started down the stairs, clutching a large Plexiglas container.

"No," Alex said automatically, throwing out his arm to shield his new nanny from harm when he saw the lid had been removed.

Unfortunately Ms. Kneivel shifted, and his hand connected with her upper arm. Knocked off balance, she reeled forward.

At the very same moment, Brady gave his brother an enthusiastic wallop between the shoulder blades. "Yeah— show her, Nick!"

As if in slow motion, Nick threw up his arms, sending ants and sand spewing through the air like confetti—most of which rained down on Ms. Kneivel's open purse. With a shriek, the woman tossed the bag to the ground. Her ill-advised action caused a number of interesting items to tumble out, including an antique snuff box, an ornate silver candy dish and a graceful jade swan.

Alex looked from the objects—which properly belonged in his living room—to Ms. Kneivel's guilty face, and swore.

"Oh," Mikey said, sounding both shocked and impressed. "Daddy said a bad, bad, *bad* word."

Five

Shay was dreaming. She knew it, but didn't care.

Stretched out on a chaise longue by the pool, she lay flat on her back while Alex's dream image loomed over her.

"I want you," he murmured, his golden eyes hazy with passion. He was dressed all in white, just as he had been the first time she'd seen him. His slacks and shirt were wrinkle free, his hair beautifully styled. He was even wearing a tie.

Shay frowned. That wasn't right. He looked far too uptight for this kind of fantasy. But then again, it was her dream, wasn't it? She could make him look any way she wanted.

She squinted with concentration.

Suddenly the shirt was gone, displaying a broad expanse of smooth, sculpted chest. His golden hair had grown an inch and become untidily mussed. A dark, dangerous haze of whiskers coated his jaw.

Ah. That was more like it.

"Oh, Shay," he whispered reverently. He stroked her throat with a slightly callused fingertip. "You're so beautiful. A goddess." His mouth closed over hers, as soft as a cloud, the movement deliciously erotic.

Shay groaned with pleasure. At his words, at his touch, at the thrilling way his lips plied hers. Heat spread through her, making her as malleable as warmed candle wax. Never before had a man made her feel so mindless, so boneless, so ripe for passion. He was a great kisser. *This* was a great dream.

Except for the rude little voice in her head. The one that refused to shut up and go away, no matter how much she willed it.

Hello, in there, it said. *Anybody home?*

Shay tried to ignore it. She parted her lips, inviting her dream lover to deepen the kiss. When nothing happened, she reached for him, her hands sliding over his warm satiny skin. Little sparks of electricity shot through her. She pulled him closer, pressed the aching tips of her breasts against him, hoping he'd take the hint.

Instead, her little voice grew more shrill.

Earth to Spenser. Wake up.

Dream Alex's image began to waver.

Dream Alex? Oh, for heaven's sake! Is that like Dream Barbie and Dream Ken? Who are you—Nightmare Skipper? Where's your self-respect? Alex Morrison doesn't even like you. If you were a weed, he'd pull you. If you were a disease, he'd eradicate you. If you were a—

All right, all right. She got the picture. With a sigh of regret, she opened her eyes—and found herself face-to-face with a trio of dripping, bug-eyed creatures.

With a violent start, she gasped and snapped upright.

Her action was met with immediate shouts of laughter.

"Hey, Shay!" Brady said, chuckling as he pushed up his swim goggles. "It's us! Brady—"

"Nick!" Nicky emerged from behind his.

"And Mikey!" It took the youngest Morrison a little longer to free his eyes, since he also happened to be dressed in an inflatable swim sweater.

"Did we scare you?" Brady asked.

The world slowly began to make sense as Shay became more fully awake. She took a deep breath to calm her racing heart, a smile slowly lighting her face as she took in the three little boys' gleeful, grinning expressions. "You sure did. I thought you were awful, bug-eyed sea monsters."

Brady's grin widened. "Really?"

"You bet."

"Cool!"

She reached up and tweaked his nose. "Twerp." She adjusted the back of the longue to a more upright position. "What are you doing here? Did you find a new nanny?"

The trio wagged their heads from side to side in perfect unison and assumed identical angelic expressions.

"Nope." Brady's tone could best be described as jolly. "Ms. Jernigan was ascared of Mikey, and Ms. Kay only liked canaries, and Daddy made Ms. Marks leave early, and Ms. Kneivel sort of got ants spilled on her by accident, and that's how we found out she tried to steal our stuff. And then when Daddy called Aunt Frannie, she said we can't have any more of her nannies 'cuz our house isn't safe. Daddy called it Nannygate."

"He said a bad word," Mikey added.

"He's been doing that a lot lately," Nick said. "Wanna hear it?"

"Ah, no." Shay already got the picture—and then some.

Brady cocked his head. "Were you having a bad dream?"

Heat crept into her cheeks. "Why do you ask?" She wasn't certain she wanted to hear the answer.

"You were making real funny noises," Nick said.

"We wanted to wake you up before," Brady informed her, "but Daddy said we shouldn't."

"Daddy?" Maybe she wasn't as awake as she thought. "Daddy who?"

All three boys chuckled as if she were making a joke.

"*Daddy,* Daddy," Mikey supplied, as Nick pointed beyond her toward the pool house.

Shay dutifully rotated her head ninety degrees to the right—and found herself gazing directly at Alex, who was standing perhaps ten feet away, one hand braced against the cabana's inner doorway.

Good heavens. Except for a pair of sunglasses and a brief black swimsuit, he was stark, staring naked!

Brilliant, Skipper. What did you expect? That he'd come to the pool in a three-piece suit?

Well, why not? That was certainly no more incredible than the discovery that his real-life near nakedness was even better than her fantasy.

But oh, it *was,* she realized, her heart doing a little bump as her gaze climbed his body. His skin, lightly tanned to a pale shade of bronze, stretched taut and sleek over the flat slabs of muscle that comprised his abdomen and chest, bisected by a fine arrow of pale brown hair, a significant improvement on what she'd imagined. But then, so was the way his hair was tousled in damp, gleaming spikes, like that of those impossibly beautiful men in the suntan lotion ads.

Only his expression was off-putting. "I thought I told you boys to leave Ms. Spenser alone and let her sleep," he said sternly.

"We did!" Brady protested.

"We were just making sure she was okay," Nick said.

"See, she was making those strange noises again," Brady started to explain, "and—"

"I woke up all by myself," Shay interrupted hastily. She wasn't sure what noises she'd made, but she was certain she didn't want the boys to reproduce them for their father. She summoned a smile for Alex. "They haven't been bothering me. Really."

"Right."

He took a step forward and the boys—the little cowards—scattered like chaff before a hurricane. "Uh, now that you're here to watch, can we get back in the water?'' Brady asked, fleeing toward the shallow end with Nick and Mikey so close that for a moment the trio looked like one boy with three heads.

''Yes,'' Alex responded tersely. ''You may.'' He stalked past Shay to drop into one of the chairs grouped around the glass-topped umbrella table a few feet to her left. His scent, a combination of fresh air, chlorine, a faint trace of after-shave and a great deal of sun-warmed man, swamped her. ''Just make sure you behave.''

He glanced in her direction. Although she couldn't see his eyes due to the sunglasses, her skin tingled as she felt his gaze play over her. He nodded toward the soft-drink can in his hand. ''Want one?'' It sounded more like an accusation than an offer.

''No.'' Her voice came out even huskier than usual. ''No thanks.''

He propped his feet on the opposite chair, popped the top on the cola and took a long swig.

In the pool, out of Alex's direct line of vision, Nick climbed on Brady's shoulders. Mugging outrageously, they struck a pose, flexed their nonexistent muscles and waved at Shay.

She gave a soft laugh and waggled her fingers at them. ''You're lucky,'' she told Alex. ''They really are great kids.''

He made a derisive sound. ''Unless you happen to make the crucial mistake of applying to be their nanny. Then they're demented.''

She tried to look serious, but it wasn't easy. ''Tough day?''

''You could say that.''

''The boys mentioned you didn't find a suitable person for the job.''

He was silent for so long Shay thought he wasn't going to answer. But then he sighed, tipped his chair back on two legs and stared at her over the top of his sunglasses. ''Not true. Except for Ms. Marks, the other three weren't that bad. Of course, I'll never know for certain, since one left convinced I'm harboring a pyromaniac, the other believes my house is infested with rabid bats and the third got a bucket of ants poured on her."

She bit her lip, certain he wouldn't take it kindly if she laughed. "I understand the last lady had a few problems of her own."

He hitched his shoulders dismissively. "It wouldn't have mattered if she'd been Mother Theresa. The boys pulled the ant trick *before* we found out she was a kleptomaniac. Bottom line, they can't be trusted."

"Maybe you just haven't found the right person."

He shook his head. "I don't think so. We've been through nine—no, make that ten—nannies in a year and a half. It's them." Across the way, Brady glanced at Alex's averted face, then scampered out of the pool and over to the garden that edged the deck, where he snapped the blooms off a huge clump of hot pink petunias, leaving nothing behind but stems.

Oblivious, Alex continued to vent steam. "They're willful and disobedient, with no respect for authority."

Shay glanced at him in disbelief. *They're smart and imaginative—and desperate for your attention.* It was so obvious, she didn't understand how he could miss it.

With another quick look in his father's direction, Brady tossed the flowers in the pool. "Hey, guys!" he called to his brothers, making a tremendous splash as he rejoined them. "Let's play X-Men! These can be our special ammo we use to blow away the Blob and the rest of the criminals! Hey, Mikey—you're the Blob!" He scooped up a handful of sodden flowers and pelted his youngest sibling with them. Mikey fired back, Nick entered the fray, and all three boys shrieked with laughter.

"They don't need a nanny," Alex concluded. "They need a handler."

They don't need a nanny, Shay decided. *They need a father.*

The question was, was there any way to get Alex to act like one? Shay didn't know, but she was willing to give it a try.

She turned thoughtfully toward him. "You know," she said, choosing her words with care, "you're right. They *are* a handful. I hadn't realized you'd been through so many nannies. Did you say ten?"

"That's right."

She shook her head. "That's terrible. Do you have any idea what you're going to do?"

He shrugged his wide shoulders. "I haven't decided."

She rested her chin on her hand. "I suppose you've considered boarding school?"

"Boarding school?"

"There are several excellent military academies on the East Coast. I did a series on them when I was first starting out. One, Markhurst, was really outstanding. I'd be happy to call the commander for you."

"I don't think so."

"I really think it might be your answer. Lord knows, Commander Kreig would get the boys whipped into shape in no time. A year or two of short-order drills, daily inspections and some real discipline might really help."

"Good Lord. Michael's only four." Alex stared at her in disbelief. "You aren't serious, are you?"

"Hey—it's only a suggestion. It's sure nothing to get bent out of shape over. I mean, *I've* never had a problem with the boys. As a matter of fact, when *I* was in charge, everything went fine." She paused, then added thoughtfully, "Children can tell when you're secure in your authority."

There was a telling pause. "Are you implying I'm not?"

"Of course not." She uttered a mental apology to the boys for what she was about to do, praying it would be worth it in the long run. "Although, they do tend to ignore what you tell them, don't they? And they can be a little...rowdy."

"Just what do you mean by that?" He bristled, suddenly as fierce as a lion defending his cubs.

"Well..." She worried her lip, then said reluctantly, "Look at the mess they're making right now. All those flowers can't be good for the filter system."

He was on his feet in a flash. "What the—!" He slapped down the pop can with an abrupt movement that sent his sunglasses crashing to the ground. "Boys! Stop that right now!"

Brady, Nick and Mikey froze. They'd added some geraniums and a sprinkling of marigolds to their munitions supply; a mixture of red, yellow and pink petals dotted the water, as well as their hair and faces. Their expressions mirrored abject surprise at their father's tone of voice. "What's the matter, Daddy?" Nick asked innocently.

Alex marched toward them, his back rigid. "You know darn well you're not supposed to put things like sticks, rocks, leaves *or flowers* in the pool!"

"But this is ammo!" Brady protested.

"I don't care what it is. I want it out. Now!"

"But, Dad—"

"Not another word," Alex interrupted. "I want that mess cleaned up and then I want you out of the pool." He folded his arms across his chest and waited.

"Well, you don't gotta have a cow about it," Brady muttered. "We wouldn't act this way if we had somebody like Shay to watch over us."

It was the wrong thing to say. Alex glared at him. "That is enough."

Brady looked from his father to his brothers, whose chins were drooping glumly, then shrugged and began to scoop up the soggy flowers. Nick and Mikey joined in, and a few minutes later they all climbed dejectedly out of the pool.

"Get your towels, go into the cabana and get cleaned up. Wait for me at the front door."

"Yes, Daddy." They trudged past Shay, the picture of woe.

She hardened her heart. Now was not the time to turn into a marshmallow. She picked up her beach bag, took out her source book, a pen and a pad of paper, and stood. She walked over to the table, where she made a show of riffling through the book and copying down a name and phone number.

"Here." She thrust the sheet of paper at Alex as he came to retrieve his sunglasses.

He took it warily. "What's this?"

"The Markhurst number."

He looked at it a long minute...and crumpled it in his fist. "I don't need it," he said curtly.

"But—"

"I've decided to reschedule my trip. It can wait a few weeks while I get the boys back on track."

"Really?" She winced at the pleased surprise in her voice, then relaxed as it became clear Alex was too caught up in his own emotions to notice. "Are you sure that's wise?"

"Absolutely. I'll give them a little refresher course on manners, remind them there are always repercussions for unacceptable behavior. By the time Aunt Frannie finds the right nanny, they'll be ready."

"Oh. Well. If there's anything I can do...?"

He shook his head. "I can handle it," he said decisively. "If you'll excuse me?"

"Oh. Of course."

He started toward the cabana, only to pause as he reached the entrance. She could see him hesitate before he turned. "Maybe there is one thing you could do."

"Sure." She tried not to sound too eager.

"You wouldn't happen to know if cats have belly buttons, would you?"

Her jaw sagged before she caught herself. "Of course they do," she said automatically. "They're mammals. You just can't see them—the belly buttons—because of the fur."

"Thanks." Without any further explanation, he turned and disappeared into the cabana.

Shay stared after him. He was prickly, autocratic, hard to like and harder to understand.

So why, *why*, did she want to get to know him better anyway? In a manner that had nothing to do with the boys... and everything to do with the man?

Was it because she'd always loved a challenge? Or because matching wits with him made her feel more alive than she felt for a long, long time?

Or was it nothing more than that damnable chemistry?

After all. He did have great buns.

You need help, Skipper, her little voice said sadly.

The worst part was, it was right. With a despairing moan for her overactive hormones, Shay walked to the deep end and threw herself headlong into the pool.

"*You're* going to take care of us?" Brady stared at Alex incredulously.

All four Morrisons were seated around the table in the informal dining room off the kitchen. Tired from the long, eventful day, Alex had again attempted toasted cheese sandwiches, this time without mishap. Then he'd waited until the end of the meal to make his announcement. He'd harbored a vague idea the boys would be so excited by his news that they might not be able to eat if he told them sooner.

Clearly, he needn't have worried. At least not where Brady was concerned. Although his eldest son didn't appear dismayed exactly, neither did he look anywhere close to thrilled, either. What he looked was... thoughtful.

He's probably revising his next nanny-disposal plan, Alex thought caustically.

"You're really going to stay with us?" Brady said.

"That's right. I realized it's been a while since we spent some quality time together."

"We never spend *any* time together," Nick said.

Alex transferred his gaze to him, surprised by the statement. "Sure we do. How about our trip to Disneyland at Christmas?"

"But Ms. Barnacle's the one that took us to see Mickey Mouse and stuff," Brady pointed out. "Remember? You stayed at the hotel to work."

"Her name was Barnstable," Alex murmured. He raised his voice. "And the important thing is not what happened in the past, but that we're going to spend some time together *now*," he stressed. "It'll be fun." And in the process, you boys are going to learn a few things.

And so will Shay Spenser.

Every time he let himself think about their most recent encounter he felt tense and out of sorts. It'd been bad enough to walk out and find her lying there, wearing nothing but that flimsy bronze-colored bathing suit. He hadn't meant to stare, but with her vibrant personality softened by sleep, she'd looked young and uncharacteristically vulnerable. And even so, he'd been moving away, shooing the boys before him, when she'd given that breathy little sigh that had reclaimed his attention.

God knew, he hadn't meant to witness the way she'd stretched languorously, molding the thin swimsuit to the erected points of her breasts. Any more than he'd intended to notice the dreamy half smile of sheer pleasure that had curved the fullness of her soft lips.

But he had.

And he'd paid. It'd taken him ten laps at a brutal pace and an icy shower to dispel the jackhammer pulse of need the sight had sent hammering through him.

And then what had she done?

Had she yelled at the boys for waking her up? Had she seemed the least bit embarrassed to have been caught napping at *his* pool? Had she done or said anything to suggest the monumentally annoying physical attraction he felt for her might possibly be mutual?

Of course not. That would be too simple. Too easy. Too humane. Too nice.

Instead, she'd suggested she was more capable of parenting his sons than he was!

Well, they'd just see about that.

"Daddy?"

"What is it, Brady?"

"You *are* going to be here for my birthday, aren't you?"

Alex considered the date still three weeks away. He supposed his trip could wait that long. Besides, he remembered how much he'd loved birthdays as a boy; he couldn't very well miss his own son's. "Of course."

"*Perfect.* Can I be excused?"

"Me, too?" Nick chimed.

Surprised by their abrupt requests, he shrugged. "Sure, I guess."

"Great!" The pair jumped up and bounded away.

Only Mikey hung back. "Daddy?" He climbed down from his chair, came around the table and sidled up beside Alex.

"What is it, Michael?"

The child crooked a finger, motioning Alex to bend his head.

Assuming the boy wanted to whisper in his ear like he had in the past, Alex leaned over.

As soft as a butterfly, Mikey bussed a kiss to his cheek. "I'm glad you're gonna be our new nanny," he said shyly.

He bolted toward the door.

Alex stared after him, his heart in a turmoil. All of the bravado that had been sustaining him since he'd made the decision to take over abruptly deserted him.

Good God. What the hell had he done?

Six

"What do you mean, she's not coming in?" Alex said into the kitchen phone first thing the next morning. He tightened his grip on the receiver. "The woman is your employee. You can order her to come to work. Or get me someone else!"

Francine Layman's voice was apologetic, but firm. "I'm sorry, Mr. Morrison. Unfortunately, the word has gone out about the problems at your house. I don't know what you expect me to do. I can't *make* Mrs. Lent—or anyone else—clean and cook for you."

"I understand that," he said with exaggerated patience, unable to believe this was happening to him. He glanced around the room. The place was a mess. It was amazing how many glasses, plates, bowls and spoons three small boys could use without ever eating a real meal. In addition, the flour and juice that had been spilled during yesterday's attempt to apprehend Brutus had been tracked all over the white tile floor, making it impossible to walk anywhere without hitting a sticky patch.

He *needed* a housekeeper, dammit. "As I said, I understand. That doesn't change the fact that we have a contract—"

"One that requires you to provide safe working conditions," she said, interrupting. "Of which, my lawyer has informed me, rat, bat, ant and spider infestations are definite violations. Besides, Mrs. Lent didn't quit. She's ill."

"Listen, Ms. Layman. As far as I'm aware, an 'attack of the vapors' hasn't been considered a viable medical illness for about a hundred years," he retorted, referring to the reason she'd given for the housekeeper's absence.

Aunt Frannie was silent a moment, then sniffed. "Do you know, Mr. Morrison," she said with great dignity, "I've never met your brother, but I'm beginning to understand why your fiancée prefers him. Now, if you'll excuse me, my other phone is ringing. Good day." To Alex's disbelief, she hung up.

With a heartfelt oath, he did, too. For one wild instant he found himself tempted to say to hell with the whole thing, call Helen and tell her to see if there was an opening at one of his resorts. The staff could watch the boys, he could work, and he wouldn't have to deal with any of this.

Of course, if he did that, the boys would probably grow up to be hellions who would terrorize innocent people until one day they wound up somewhere a whole lot worse than some military academy.

The thought was like a splash of cold water. It was that—and not his determination to prove to a certain little brunette that he could handle things—that made him take himself firmly in hand. He took a deep breath, clamped down on his panicky emotions and forced himself to consider the situation rationally.

The moment he did, he could see that this latest development was actually more an inconvenience than a calamity. After all, Mrs. Rosencrantz, his regular housekeeper, would be back from vacation in two and a half weeks. Although he might not have any great experience running a house, it couldn't be that different from running a business, at which he excelled.

The first thing to do was get organized, something he could start on right now. He took another long look around, only this time he started a mental list. *Clean kitchen* was right at the top. Next he made a methodical search of the refrigerator, freezer and pantry, considered his cooking skills—toasted cheese sandwiches comprised his repertoire—and added *go to store/buy frozen food*.

Brady chose that moment to wander in, followed by Nick and Mikey. Feet dragging, hair standing on end, small faces smudged with sleep, all three boys shuffled over and climbed up onto the stools that lined one side of the tiled cooking island.

"'Morning, Daddy," they mumbled, yawning.

"Good morning." He started to fill the sink with hot water, then stopped. He regarded the threesome speculatively.

If he acted wisely, he could use Mrs. Lent's desertion to his advantage, he thought slowly. Her absence would certainly give him lots of opportunities to teach the boys a sense of responsibility. And it would prove to Shay beyond any doubt that he was on top of things.

Not that her opinion mattered, he told himself hastily. It didn't. She'd merely pointed out there was a problem. It was how he took care of it that was important.

"I'm glad you boys are up," he said decisively, feeling back in control. "We have lots to do today."

"Oh, boy! Are you gonna take us out on the boat?" Nick asked.

"Shay could come," Brady added eagerly. "She knows all about boats and—"

"No." Alex shook his head. "I've got something else in mind. Mrs. Lent isn't coming, so we're going to have to take care of ourselves. We're going to start by getting this kitchen whipped into shape. Then we'll go to the grocery store and stock up on things to eat."

" 'Kay," said Mikey amiably.

Brady and Nick, however, stared at him in dismay.

"Now? But we just waked up," Brady said.

"We haven't even had breakfast yet," Nick picked up the protest.

"Yeah." Brady nodded up and down. "When Shay was here, she *always* fixed us breakfast. Really good breakfast. And she took us places. Cool places. Like to the beach to fly kites. And to the airport to watch the planes land and take off."

Alex's eyes narrowed. "Well, *I'm* taking you to the store. As for breakfast—" Hell. He already knew there wasn't an egg, piece of fruit or box of cereal to be found in the place.

Shay had undoubtedly depleted the supply while being a paragon.

He refused to admit defeat, however. He thought for a second, then grabbed three plates and yanked the leftover pizza he'd brought home from Letsa Eatsa Pizza out of the fridge. With a flourish and a look that dared the boys to protest, he served them each a slice. "There." He dusted off his hands.

"Hey, cool," Nick said in surprise. Mikey nodded in agreement and even Brady looked impressed.

Alex felt a ridiculous pang of pleasure. That was good, because he needed it to sustain him through the next two hours and forty minutes, which was how long it took the boys to finish breakfast, get dressed, make their beds and help him clean the kitchen, a job he could have done alone in twenty-five minutes.

Eventually, however, the counters were clean and uncluttered, the floor spick-and-span, the spices restored to the rack and the pizza box relegated to the proper recycling bin. Alex put one last dirty bowl in the dishwasher, took note of the tomato sauce stains on his shirt and dried his hands on a dish towel. He regarded his helpers. "Good job," he said with a nod of approval. "All that's left to do is put in the soap."

Brady darted around him and yanked open the sink cabinet. "Can I do it, Daddy? Please? I've seen Mrs. Rosencrantz do it a zillion times."

"Sure. While you're at it, I'll go change my shirt." His spirits buoyed by the way the morning had gone, he took the stairs two at a time. This wasn't so hard after all.

When he came downstairs, he found the boys had already gone outside to wait for him. He hurriedly set the dishwasher on delayed wash, locked the house and loaded everyone into the car, which had been fixed earlier that morning. It started right up, thanks to Arnie.

After a quick trip to a burger joint for lunch, they arrived at the grocery store at half past one. Alex herded the boys inside and instructed them to stay close, then grabbed a cart and loaded up on cereal, bread and milk, before heading for the frozen food section.

It had been a long time since he'd done his own shopping, and the selection was truly amazing. He stared in amazement at row after row of prepared foods that ranged from egg rolls to chicken nuggets to pumpkin pie. There were even breakfasts that included eggs, pancakes and sausage, in clever little boxes that could go into the microwave. Where meals were concerned, the next two weeks should be a piece of cake.

Brady tugged on his shirt sleeve. "Daddy?"

"What?"

"Can me and the guys go over and look at the live lobster tank?"

Alex glanced in the direction Brady indicated, contemplated the murky container of pincher-waving creatures in the seafood deli and nodded, although he felt compelled to add a precautionary statement. "Yes. Just don't touch anything."

"'Kay!" Off they raced, the two older boys neck and neck, Mikey right behind them.

Alex moved down toward the opposite end of the aisle. He started to toss a handful of TV dinners into the cart, only to falter when an amused voice said, "Ah. Into nutrition, I see."

His body tightened instantly as he recognized Shay's husky voice. Disgruntled—what was it about her that had such an undignified effect on him?—he dropped the dinners on top of his other selections, jerked around and said, "What're you doing here?"

Her eyes widened at his tone. "I'm not late, am I?"

She looked cool and delectable in white shorts, a peach-colored blouse and sandals that showed the firm curves of her slender legs to definite advantage. Despite the chill coming off the refrigeration units, a blast of heat rolled through him. "Late for what?" He knew he was being rude, but he couldn't seem to help it.

She tipped her head, her expression quizzical. "To catch a ride home. When Brady called—"

"Wait a minute. Brady called you? When?"

Her look of puzzlement deepened. "A little over an hour ago."

Right about the time Alex had gone to change his shirt. "Why?"

"To ask if I needed anything from the store. When I explained I was bringing my car in to be serviced, he told me to hold on, then came back on the line and said you'd be happy to give me a lift home. I just assumed..." She trailed off as she saw the look on his face. "He didn't talk to you, did he?" He shook his head and she started to back away. "Oh. Well. Don't worry about it, okay? I'm sure one of the guys from the garage will be happy to give me a lift."

His gaze strayed from the pansylike depths of her eyes to the creamy fullness of her lips. He just bet they would. "Forget it."

She stopped in surprise. "What?"

"The gate is closed," he said gruffly. "You couldn't get in. Besides, it's no problem." His sense of fair play dictated the answer. After all, even if she was too brash, too confident, too—his mouth twisted as the word *underclothed* came to mind—for his taste, she'd been good to the boys and she was Beau's friend. Plus, she'd been nice enough to drive to dinner the other night. The least he could do was return the favor.

"Thanks."

"Forget it," he said again. "It's not a big deal."

There was a charged silence as their gazes met and held. A slight flush stained Shay's cheeks, and she abruptly glanced away, scanning the contents of his cart. "Brady mentioned Mrs. Lent had left you in the lurch. It looks like you don't expect her back anytime soon."

He grabbed blindly at another handful of dinners. "True."

"I have to admit, I was surprised when he said you were going grocery shopping. I half expected you to pack up and head to one of your resorts or something."

He gave a guilty start. What was she—psychic? "Haven't you heard? The world isn't the same as it was when you and I were kids. Women can be roving reporters—" which would be a damn good thing for him to remember "—and men can be Mr. Mom. Times have changed."

"They have, haven't they?" Her eyes sparkled impishly. "Lord knows, I don't think my father has ever seen the inside of a grocery store." She chuckled, a low raspy sound that went straight to Alex's gut.

He glanced down and saw he had a stranglehold on a bag of frozen corn. He loosened his grip and forced himself to focus on what she'd said. "Not the domestic type, huh?"

"Hardly."

There was something in her tone—a touch of asperity underlying the more obvious fondness—that plucked at his curiosity. "Is he an adventurer like you?"

"Good grief, no. He can barely remember to eat, much less shop. He's a genetic researcher. Cautious, methodical, dedicated—the stereotypical absentminded scientist. He never remembers a birthday, an anniversary or a holiday, but he can talk for days about DNA sequencing.''

Alex didn't know quite what to say, so he settled on the obvious. ''That must've been hard on your mom.''

''I don't think so,'' she said dryly. ''You see, she's a geneticist, too, and she's every bit as absorbed in her work as my dad is.'' She fell into step beside him as he moved toward the juice section. ''They love to tell the story about how they meant to name me Sharon, but got distracted in the middle of explaining to the recording nurse how to spell it. They told her the first three letters, and then my mother turned to my dad and asked him *why* he thought a particular experiment of hers had failed, forgetting the poor nurse was even there. That's how I became Shay, *S-H-A—Y.*'' She shook her head ruefully. ''I love them dearly, but they're fanatics when it comes to their work.''

Alex was silent. It was the last sort of background he would ever have imagined for her. ''So who raised you?''

She shrugged. ''Housekeepers. Baby-sitters. Teachers. My friends' parents. Once I got to my teens, I pretty much raised myself.''

''No brothers or sisters?''

''No.'' A wistful expression crossed her face. ''I think that's one of the reasons I enjoy Brady, Mikey and Nick so much. They don't always get along, but they stick up for each other. It's really nice to watch.'' She glanced around. ''Where are they, anyway?''

He nodded toward the seafood section. ''They're over there looking at the lobsters.''

''Alone?'' She twisted around.

His gaze dropped. To his disgust he realized he was checking the ripe curve of her derriere for a panty line. ''Yes, alone.'' He turned his attention to the boys. ''And before you say something— don't. I can see them from here, so they're perfectly safe. And they're behaving for once, not touching anything, exactly the way I told them. See? There's Mikey by the clam sauce display. And Brady is simply

standing by the tank, talking to Nick, who's—what the heck
is Nick doing?''

"Why, it looks like he's—ohmigosh! Alex, I think he's
unscrewing the drain plug!'' She took off at a run.

Alex stood frozen to the spot for all of half a second, before he sprang into action and bounded after her. With his
longer legs, he quickly passed her. "Nicholas," he roared.
"Don't touch that—"

The admonition came too late. With a terrible gurgle,
water began to spurt out of the opened drain. Alex hit the
brakes, only to slip on the shiny linoleum floor. Backped-
aling wildly, he slid directly toward the tank.

He arrived right in time to catch the full force of the flood
square in the face.

Nobody spoke a word on the way home.

Wisely so, since Alex was pretty darn angry and didn't
care who knew it.

Not that he didn't have just cause. In addition to being
soaked from head to toe and smelling like the bottom of a
dirty fishbowl, he was out $662.00 for Nick's little misad-
venture—$262.00 for groceries and $400.00 for damages.

Adding insult to injury, when he'd asked the boy why he'd
done such a thing, the six-year-old's reply had been an un-
satisfactory, "Gee, Daddy, because Brady told me to."

When Alex had turned on Brady, his eldest son had widened his eyes innocently and said, "Well, gosh. I just wondered if all that water could really come out of such a little
hole."

As bad as that was, it wasn't even the worst of it.

The really aggravating part was that on top of everything
else, Alex had left his checkbook at home. So, although he'd
had enough cash for the groceries, he'd been forced to borrow the rest from the woman currently sitting beside him.

The one whose mouth kept twitching as she stared fixedly out the window. The one who'd had to bite her lip in
the store to keep a straight face when she'd handed him four

crisp one-hundred-dollar bills. The very same woman who'd sounded almost as guileless as his sons when she'd said, "Gee, it's sure lucky the way this worked out. Usually, I don't have this much cash on me."

That was when he'd realized she was lending him the very same money he'd given her the day they'd met.

Staring straight ahead, Alex felt something tug at him that wasn't quite anger. In fact, it felt dangerously like a prickle of amusement as the absurdity of the incident struck him.

He wasn't about to give in to it, however. He could just imagine the sort of diabolical thing the boys would do next if they thought he wasn't totally disgusted with their behavior. It didn't bear consideration, he told himself, as he used the remote on the gate, followed the drive around to the portico off the kitchen, stopped the car and turned off the engine.

"If nobody minds," he said coolly, "I'd like to ditch these wet clothes in the mudroom."

"What about the groceries?" Shay asked.

He gave her a sour look. "Why don't you give me a minute and I'll come back and unload them."

Shay cleared her throat. "Good idea. I'll keep an eye on the boys."

"Good luck," he muttered under his breath.

Startled by that unexpected flash of humor, she watched him stride over and unlock the back door. She could hear his shoes squish with every step, and even though a part of her wanted desperately to laugh, another part of her felt overwhelmed by admiration for the way he'd handled himself today.

As mad as he'd been after his dousing, he hadn't yelled at the boys or berated them. In fact, his first concern had been for their safety. And once he'd been assured of that, he'd managed, even as embarrassed as he'd been, to be civil both to the store manager and the rest of the employees. He hadn't quibbled about money or tried to pin the blame for Nick's misdeed on anyone else, either.

He'd been the very definition of grace under fire. She had to admit she was impressed.

She was also surprised by how easy he'd been to talk to. Heaven knew, she didn't normally go around boring people with the details of her childhood. But then, in the world she'd inhabited for more than a decade, it was the story that was important, not the reporter.

A fact that hadn't mattered until today. With Alex.

"Shay?"

She twisted around to regard Brady and his brothers. "Hmm?"

"Do you think Daddy will ever forgive us?"

Her mouth quirked. The boy had a definite flair for the melodramatic, she thought wryly. "Of course he will. Even though that was a pretty dumb thing you guys did." She tried to look stern. "Dumb for Nick to do, and dumb for you to encourage. Someone could've been hurt."

Brady nodded soberly. "Like Daddy almost was." Although his expression was exceedingly solemn, Shay could've sworn she saw something calculated come and go in his big brown eyes for an instant. "He's trying really hard to take good care of us, but it's not easy, 'cuz he's all alone. I think that's why he looked so sad yesterday when we came in from the pool."

"He did?" Shay said in surprise.

"He did?" Nick echoed.

Brady sent his brother a pointed look, prompting the younger boy to suddenly sit up straight and say, "Oh, yeah." He nodded vigorously. "He did."

"That's right," Brady continued smoothly. "Real sad. Uncle Beau says ever since Mommy went to heaven, Daddy's been real lonesome and that he needs someone who—"

"BRADY!"

All four of them jumped as Alex's irate voice shattered the hushed atmosphere in the car.

"Uh-oh," Brady said apprehensively. "I wonder what's the matter now."

"You boys stay here and I'll go find out," Shay hastily volunteered. It was only fair since, much to her shame, what she really wanted to do was stay right there and pump Brady about what Beau had said. It was hardly a noble ambition, and it certainly wasn't a good example to set for the children.

With any luck at all, a good dose of Alex being surly would cure her of such unheroic curiosity, she thought, climbing out of the car. She'd go check things out, be re-reminded of all the negative things she'd previously observed about his personality, and no doubt this brief bout of ill-advised interest would be dispelled. She hurried toward the house and into the mudroom, which opened onto the kitchen.

"Alex? What's wrong?" she asked, only to gasp as she glanced toward the adjoining room and saw it was ankle-high in bubbles.

But that wasn't what stopped her in her tracks. What stopped her was Alex—and the discovery that he'd already stripped off most of his wet clothes.

Shay knew it was rude to stare, but she couldn't help it.

There was a definite difference between the way a man looked in a swimsuit, she decided as her gaze slowly slid from Alex's chest to his navel to points south, and the way he looked in wet white silk boxer shorts. For one thing—a big thing, she thought before she could catch herself—the damp shorts clung like plastic wrap and were nearly as transparent.

Alex must have realized the same thing, because suddenly he made a strangled sound, snatched up his pants and held them in front of him like a shield. "What the devil are you doing in here!"

"I—I came to help."

"Yeah?" he bit out. "Well, I don't need any help."

"I n-noticed."

One dark eyebrow shot up. "What do you mean by that?" he demanded.

"Nothing. I just—you just—but then I saw—I mean—"

"Hell! I don't believe this!" To her shock, he gave her a long, hard look and tossed his slacks to the floor with a growl of frustration. "You want to look? Be my guest. And if you like *that* so much—" in two long strides, he closed the space between them "—how about *this?*"

Faster than she could blink, he reached out, hauled her into his arms and fastened his mouth to hers.

It was...heavenly. With a moan of sheer exhilaration, Shay reached up, clutched his wide shoulders and molded herself against him.

Her little voice went crazy. *Stop that this instant! You're being utterly shameless! This sort of behavior will only bring you—*

Pleasure. Pure, unadulterated, overpowering pleasure. It swept through her veins like a trail of dynamite, blowing away her inhibitions. Whimpering, she not only opened her mouth for his tongue, she plastered herself even closer to his lean, powerful body, glorying in the undeniable, unmistakable proof that he was aroused, too.

He stilled for all of a nanosecond, as if stunned by her ardent response. Then he wrapped his arms even tighter around her, so that every shuddering breath he took rubbed his chest against her nipples. He slanted his head, deepening the angle of the kiss and began to knead the curve of her bottom with his hands.

The sensation was the most erotic thing she'd ever experienced. She whimpered. It was delicious. It was luscious. It was—

Gone. Gone, as Alex gave a giant shudder and released her as if she were a live wire.

Totally unprepared for his sudden move, she staggered at the sudden loss of support, her watery knees threatening to dump her to the floor.

PLAY
ONE MILLION
BIG BUCK$
ONE MILLION
AND YOU COULD WIN THE
$1,000,000.00
PLUS JACKPOT!
YOUR PERSONAL GAME CARD INSIDE . . .
SILHOUETTE

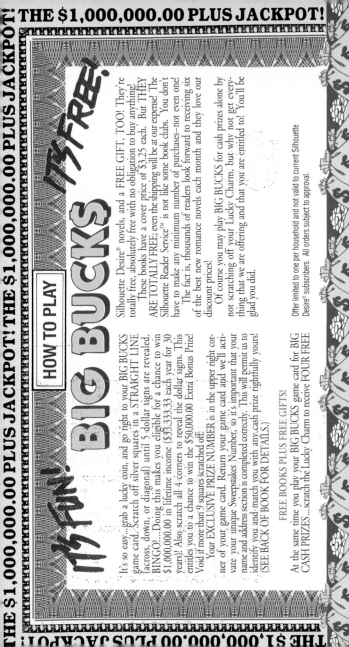

IT'S FUN! BIG BUCK$ IT'S FREE!

HOW TO PLAY

It's so easy...grab a lucky coin, and go right to your BIG BUCKS game card. Scratch off silver squares in a STRAIGHT LINE (across, down, or diagonal) until 5-dollar signs are revealed. BINGO!...Doing this makes you eligible for a chance to win $1,000,000.00 in lifetime income ($33,333.33 each year for 30 years)! Also scratch all 4-corners to reveal the dollar signs. This entitles you to a chance to win the $50,000.00 Extra Bonus Prize! Void if more than 9 squares scratched off.

Your EXCLUSIVE PRIZE NUMBER is in the upper right corner of your game card. Return your game card and we'll activate your unique Sweepstakes Number; so it's important that your name and address section is completed correctly. This will permit us to identify you and-match you with any cash prize rightfully yours! (SEE BACK OF BOOK FOR DETAILS.)

FREE BOOKS PLUS FREE GIFTS!

At the same time you play your BIG BUCKS game card for BIG CASH PRIZES...scratch the Lucky Charm to receive FOUR FREE

Silhouette Desire® novels, and a FREE GIFT, TOO! They're totally free, absolutely free with no obligation to buy anything! These books have a cover price of $3.25 each. But THEY ARE TOTALLY FREE; even the shipping will be at our expense! The Silhouette Reader Service™ is not like some book clubs. You don't have to make any minimum number of purchases–not even one!

The fact is, thousands of readers look forward to receiving six of the best new romance novels each month and they love our discount prices!

Of course you may play BIG BUCKS for cash prizes alone by not scratching off your Lucky Charm, but why not get everything that we are offering and that you are entitled to! You'll be glad you did.

Offer limited to one per household and not valid to current Silhouette Desire® subscribers. All orders subject to approval.

EXCLUSIVE PRIZE # 31 018049

BIG BUCK$

$

HURRY!
This jackpot must be claimed!
Scratch Here ➘

LUCKY CHARM GAME!
Claim
4 FREE books
AND a FREE
Mystery Gift!

YES! I have played my BIG BUCKS game card as instructed. Enter my Big Bucks Prize number in the MILLION DOLLAR Sweepstakes III and also enter me for the Extra Bonus Prize. When winners are selected, tell me if I've won. If the Lucky Charm is scratched off, I will also receive everything revealed, as explained on the back of this page.

225 CIS AS3M
(U-SIL-D-07/95)

NAME _____

ADDRESS _____ APT. _____

CITY _____ STATE _____ ZIP _____

NO PURCHASE OR OBLIGATION NECESSARY TO ENTER SWEEPSTAKES.

© 1993 HARLEQUIN ENTERPRISES LTD.   PRINTED IN U.S.A.

TWO WAYS TO WIN BIG BUCKS!

1. Uncover 5 $ signs in a row . . . BINGO! You're eligible for a chance to win the $1,000,000.00 SWEEPSTAKES!

2. Uncover 5 $ signs in a row AND uncover $ signs in all 4 corners . . . BINGO! You're also eligible for a chance to win the $50,000.00 EXTRA BONUS PRIZE!

He lunged toward her, caught her elbow and held her up. "Damn!" he said tersely. "That was—I didn't mean—aw, damn!" He raked his fingers through his hair. "I don't know what came over me! It's just—*everything.*" He pivoted away, gesturing at the pond of bubbles in his kitchen. "Hell—look at this place!"

Shay stared at his broad, beautiful back. She tried to think of something consoling to say, although she'd be the first to admit she felt pretty dazed herself.

"Well," she finally murmured. "Look on the bright side. At least, now, you won't need a shower."

Despite Shay's observation, Alex did shower.

And shave, blow dry his hair, trim his fingernails and brush and floss his teeth. He also took an inordinate amount of time deciding on the right thing to wear before he settled on khaki slacks and a pale yellow polo shirt.

Once dressed, he remade his bed and straightened the shoes on the rack in his closet. Then he got a towel and dusted off his dresser and nightstands. When that was done, he padded back into the bathroom to check his hair.

He made a face at his reflection. *This is really stupid, Morrison. Go downstairs. You're too old to be embarrassed. So what if the lady caught you without your pants? So what if you kissed her? It's not as if you haven't been with a woman or two since Allison died.*

Not that he had any intention of pursuing *that* kind of intimate relationship with Shay. He didn't. After all, despite that ill-advised kiss, he had a rule about mixing sex with his family life, and thanks to Shay's friendship with the boys and Beau, she was definitely part of the latter—whether he liked it or not.

Not that he didn't like it. He didn't care, one way or the other. Did he?

Of course not. Although, he had to admit, there had been a second or two downstairs when his hands-off policy had seemed pretty confining. But then, so had his boxer shorts.

He couldn't remember a time he'd ever felt so carnal. So greedy. So totally, quickly, completely aroused. . . .

He gave a snort of self-disgust. Dammit, he was not going to dwell on it. It was simply one more irksome event in a string of similarly annoying incidents, from having his car run out of gas to incurring the wrath of one housekeeper, four potential nannies and the head of an employment agency. Not to mention having root beer dumped in his lap and nearly becoming a new statistic—first person to drown in a grocery store. Hell, even his dishwasher had turned against him.

None of which would have seemed so bad if Shay hadn't been right at hand to witness each and every disaster. . . .

Not that *her* opinion mattered.

It didn't.

So why was he standing around up here like some spineless coward?

He wasn't, he thought decisively—at least, not any longer. Straightening his shoulders, he headed for the door.

He didn't know what he expected to see when he walked into the kitchen, but it wasn't what he found. The floor had been mopped, the groceries put away and the dishwasher emptied. The boys were sitting quietly at the counter, coloring.

Alone.

"Where's Shay?" he asked, after a casual perusal of the pantry and the anteroom.

Brady looked up from his picture. "She went home."

"She did?"

"Uh-huh."

"She left you a note." He pointed to a sheet of paper on the counter.

Alex walked over and picked it up.

Alex— Thanks for the ride. Sorry for any inconvenience. The boys were getting hungry, so I tossed to-

gether a casserole and put it and some rolls in the oven.
Hope that's okay.

Shay.

Well, heck. Wonder Woman had struck again.

And wasn't it just his luck that she'd taken off before he'd
had a chance to show her how totally unconcerned he was
about what had happened earlier?

Damn straight it was.

He shook his head and decided to take a page from Shay's
book and try to look on the bright side. At least he was going to get a homemade meal out of this. He sniffed; the
aroma from the oven was tantalizing. "Did she say what she
made for dinner?"

"Uh-huh." Brady picked up his crayon and went back to
work. "Seafood Surprise."

Alex lost his appetite.

Seven

_____

Dateline: July 22

To: Beau Morrison
    Correspondent, World News International
        Magazine
    c/o Casablanca News Desk
    Micromini cassette No. 3

Hey, Uncle Beau, I'm sorry I haven't sent you a tape
for a while, but I've been so-o-o busy. Getting a mom
is a really big job and takes lots and lots of planning.
I'm not complaining, though, 'cuz Daddy really appreciates all the help I've been giving him. He says that
if it weren't for me, his life would be dull and boring!

I know you're going to be real happy to hear that
Operation Mommy is going great. With my help,
Daddy and Shay have been together every day, and I
can tell they like each other from all the nice things they
say. Yesterday, Daddy told Shay that for a lady who

didn't have any little kids of her own, she sure knew a lot! And Shay told Daddy he could stop pretending to be perfect anytime he wanted to.

I wish they'd hurry up and decide to get married, though, 'cuz Daddy doesn't make a very good nanny. He lets us eat pizza almost every night. And when we ran out of clean clothes, he told Nick it was okay to wear his old underwear inside out because no one would ever know. He even forgot Mikey at the drugstore yesterday. We got all the way to the Burger Bar before Daddy noticed he wasn't in the car.

I guess that's okay, though, 'cuz he gave me and Nick five bucks each not to tell Shay—so *now* we have money for a wedding cake! Do you think that's enough to get one of those really cool ones with a fountain? I sure hope so.

Uh-oh, I have to go. I hear Daddy coming down the hall. I'm supposed to be resting, even though I'm not sleepy. How come when grown-ups get tired, it's always the kids who have to go to bed? I'll have to ask Shay. She'll know. She knows everything! Bye for now—Brady.

P.S. Don't forget! The big day is only ten days away!

The cottage phone was ringing.

Shay could hear the shrill, insistent *brrr* as she jogged into the front yard. Eager to get in out of the late-afternoon sun, she picked up her pace, bounded onto the porch and into the house.

She snatched up the receiver. "Hello?" She grimaced at how winded she sounded. But then, she hadn't had much time to exercise the past two weeks. One way or the other, her time had been taken up with other things.

As if on cue, Brady's voice filled her ear. "Shay? Where were you? The phone rang and rang. I didn't think you were ever gonna answer." He was talking so rapidly it took her a moment to sort out what he'd said.

"I went for a run." A trickle of perspiration tickled her temple. She looked around, then walked toward the couch. Stretching the phone cord as far as it would reach, she grabbed an old sweatshirt to mop her face.

"Can you come here? To our house?"

Her hand stilled. "What's the matter this time?"

"It's Mikey. Daddy made him take a nap, and he kind of took Tic and Tac to bed with him and now—" he paused dramatically "— they won't wake up."

That wasn't too surprising, given that Tic and Tac were— or had been—goldfish. "Brady, sweetie, I'm sorry. But I don't think—"

"Please?" he pleaded. "For poor, poor Mikey? He really loves Tic and Tac. With Brutus gone..." His voice trailed off, allowing her ample time to imagine poor Mikey's bereft face contemplating his dead-as-a-doornail goldfish. "Please? We really, really need you."

She sighed. There was no way she could say no to that kind of entreaty. Brady knew it, too, the scamp. "Okay. I'm on my way."

"Good." He hung up immediately, as if afraid if he gave her time to think she'd refuse to come.

Which is exactly what she should do, she acknowledged, as she tossed the sweatshirt back on the couch and headed out the door. And what she'd sworn she was *going* to do, after she and Alex had shared that unexpected kiss. From now on, she'd told herself, she was going to keep her distance. It was the logical, sensible thing to do.

Except that where Morrisons of any age were concerned, she was not logical, sensible nor possessed of much in the way of self-restraint. She'd started to realize that the very next day, when Brady, Mikey and Nick had arrived at her doorstep, lugging a lumpy pillowcase filled with dirty laundry they'd asked her to wash "so Daddy won't be mad at us." They'd gone on to explain how their washer and dryer had been destroyed when they'd used the appliances to polish their rock collection. Shay had taken one look at their pleading faces and felt her resolve dissolve faster than a graham cracker in milk.

As she'd suspected he might, however, Alex had taken a dim view of his sons coming to her for such personalized assistance. He'd been ... perturbed, and that's when Shay had made her next big mistake. In an attempt to downplay the episode's significance, she'd said lightly, "Relax, Alex. I've already seen your underwear, remember? Trust me, it was nothing to get excited about."

It hadn't taken more than a glance at his frigid expression to know that hadn't come out quite the way she'd intended.

The strain between them hadn't improved when she'd jogged past the house the next afternoon as he'd walked out to greet the appliance installer, either. Shay had waved. Alex had reluctantly turned to wave back—and promptly taken a barrage of water balloons in the face from the boys. For some unfathomable reason, he'd blamed *her* for his inattention.

It had taken a near disaster to effect a preliminary truce. That had happened sooner, rather than later, when Shay received a garbled call from Nick inviting her to attend the maiden voyage of the boys' hot air balloon. She'd sprinted to the house and alerted Alex, who'd gone barreling up the stairs to snatch Mikey, the pilot, to safety, seconds before the balloon was propelled off the balcony by Nick and Brady.

A subsequent inspection of the craft had shown it was a model of ingenuity, consisting of a king-size sheet tied to a plastic laundry basket, powered by a battery-operated personal fan. Alex and Shay had looked from it, to the boys, to each other, and had shared a moment of perfect understanding regarding the warped genius of the preteen mind.

That had been the start of ... something.

Something that had been nominally more civil, though still wary, when Shay had been on her way to the pool the next day and had heard a woman's frantic screams. She'd burst into the kitchen to find Alex trying futilely to calm an overwrought Mrs. Lent, who'd returned to work only to encounter Brutus cavorting in the pantry. With Shay's help, the woman had eventually calmed down, although she'd promptly announced she quit . . . forever.

And *something* that had come to resemble an unspoken alliance as they'd coped with Nick's line drive through the front window, the impressive *X-Men Ride a Dinosaur* mural the boys had done on the living room wall, and a mind-boggling number of overflowing sinks, bathtubs and toilets. It had held when they'd been reunited with old friends in the fire department after the boys tried an ill-advised experiment on the deck involving dried grass, the hot summer sun and a magnifying glass. And warmed temporarily when they'd banded together after the boys turned up missing and they found them down by the road, Nick clutching a mason jar filled with grasshoppers, while Brady waved a sign that read Wach Kid Et Live Bug—$1.00. Mikey, of course, had been the designated diner.

Unbidden, a brief smile curved Shay's mouth as she trotted along the path that led toward the house. Chances were, this newest crisis wasn't any more serious than the others. If she had a brain in her head—or an ounce of self-control—she'd stay away and let Alex handle it. Yet, she just . . . couldn't.

Partly because of Brady's heartfelt plea. Partly because she felt a responsibility to help since it had been her maneuvering that had prompted Alex to play bachelor father in the first place.

But mostly because of that *something* happening between them. Something that was careful, watchful and polite—and hummed with invisible electricity like a high-voltage line.

She shook her head as she emerged from the trees. As expected, Brady was waiting impatiently at the front door. "Come on," he said in a loud whisper, gesturing for her to hurry. The moment she was close enough, he grabbed her hand and pulled her into the shadowy foyer.

"Brady?"

"What?" He headed for the stairs, towing her behind him.

"Why are we whispering?"

"'Cuz. Mikey and Nick are asleeping."

She faltered. "But I thought you wanted me to talk to Mikey. To try and make him feel better."

"Nuh-uh." He shook his head and tugged on her hand.

She dutifully resumed climbing stairs. "What, then?"

"I want you to talk to Daddy."

Shay stopped cold and pulled the child around to face her. *"What?"*

"Shh." He motioned for her to speak more quietly.

She frowned at him but lowered her voice. "What are you talking about?"

"Daddy's gonna tell Mikey that Tic and Tac are dead. You've got to stop him."

"Brady, I can't do that."

"Why not?"

"Because I can't tell your father what to do, that's why!"

"But you've got to," Brady said earnestly. "Otherwise, Mikey's gonna think he's a murderer!"

"Come on now, Brady, don't you think you're exaggerating? Your dad wouldn't—"

"What?" interjected a loud masculine voice. "Ground an eight-year-old for life?"

Shay looked up and there was Alex. Her pulse rate jumped while her stomach sank. "Hi," she said with a weak smile.

"Hi, yourself."

He looked as scrumptious as ever in a green polo shirt and white shorts. His thick, straight hair was a little longer than it had been when they'd first met, but his golden eyes were every bit as intense and his lean cheeks as cleanly shaved. He even smelled delicious, a combination of shampoo, warm skin and a subtly delicious hint of after-shave.

She contrasted that with her own appearance, suddenly conscious of how casual her blue running shorts and over-size crop top were. Not only that, but her hair was caught back with a sweatband and her skin was still damp from her run. She didn't smell like a field of wildflowers, either.

"You want to tell me what's going on?"

"Not especially," she answered truthfully. It was proba-bly silly, but she was afraid his feelings would be hurt if he knew what Brady thought him capable of.

"I hate to break this to you, but when you get caught sneaking around somebody's house and they ask if you'd like to give an explanation, 'not especially' is *not* an ac-ceptable answer."

She sighed. "I wasn't sneaking. Brady invited me."

"Yeah, I figured that." He motioned the two of them down the stairs in front of him. "Why don't we step into my study? And then you—" the look he turned on his oldest child was not a pleasant one "—can tell me what you've done this time."

His tone had the sort of overly polite edge to it that would have worried Shay last week. Now, however, she knew his bark was as bad as it got. Even so, with Brady glued to her side, gazing at her trustingly, she felt compelled to say, "Brady didn't do anything wrong, Alex. He's just con-cerned about Mikey."

"That's what he told Ms. Jernigan," Alex murmured. At Shay's puzzled look, he added, "Forget it. Tell me why you're here."

"Is it true Mikey's goldfish have . . . expired?"

"That's right."

"Well, you see, Brady thought . . . That is . . ." This was even more awkward than she'd anticipated. "What do you plan to do about it?" she hedged.

"Well, we're not having a wake, if that's what you two are planning," he said decisively.

"Oh, no! No. We just wondered what you're going to say to Mikey."

"That's easy." He didn't try to conceal his impatience. "I'm going to tell him I'm very sorry, but due to an unfortunate accident, his goldfish are dead."

Brady shot Shay a triumphant look. "See? I told you!"

She didn't try to hide her dismay. "But Alex, you can't do that."

"Why not?" he countered, his expression guarded. "It's the truth."

"But—but—" she sputtered, trying to think of a way to dispute that particular bit of logic. "But he's just a little kid!"

"Nothing lives forever," he said flatly. "The sooner the boys learn that, the sooner they'll realize why it's best not to get too attached to anything."

She stared at him, taken aback by the callousness of the statement. It didn't jibe with the man she'd come to know in the past few weeks. All of a sudden she had the feeling that he'd just told her something important, if only she were smart enough to figure out what it was.

A dull flush warmed his cheeks at her speculative look. "Well? What do you expect me to say?" he demanded, wheeling around and pacing away. "Am I supposed to lie? Say his fish got up early and went to SeaWorld on a vacation?"

Ah. It wasn't that he *wanted* to tell Mikey the painful truth; it was that he couldn't see an alternative.

Well, she could take care of that. "If there was a solution that would eliminate the need to say anything at all—except to remind Mikey that water is an essential requirement for fish survival—would you go along?"

He turned and walked back to her. "What do you think?" He raked his fingers through his hair, and Shay had to clasp her hands together against the urge to reach up and smooth the thick, ruffled strands. "But I don't know what you can do that I haven't. Trust me," his voice turned sarcastic, "I tried everything short of CPR to bring back those fish."

"I'm not going to try to revive them," she said wryly. "I'm going to *replace* them. That is, if you'll lend me five bucks and let me borrow Brady and your car. If I leave right now, I should be able to get to the pet store in town and back before Mikey wakes up."

He stared at her, his eyes narrowed on her face. For half a second she would've sworn she saw something hot and needy burning in those golden depths. And something more—a trace of admiration, a touch of affection.

Before she could decide for sure, the moment passed as he turned and again paced away. "Damn," he said vehemently. "Why didn't I think of that?"

"Don't sweat it." For some reason her heart was pounding and her skin felt tight. "You can't think of everything."

"Yeah, Daddy," Brady piped up. He beamed at the pair of them like a proud papa whose children had done something exceedingly clever. "That's why we've got Shay."

The cottage phone was ringing.

Shay groaned, opened one eye and blinked at the pale dawn light slanting in the cottage windows. For half a second she tensed, her stomach somersaulting as she wondered what new world catastrophe she was about to be asked to cover, before her muzzy thoughts cleared enough for her to remember that she was done with that part of her life.

Relief flooded her. She looked sleepily around.

It was morning. Barely. Definitely too soon to get up. Particularly when she'd lain awake so long last night, thinking, thinking, thinking, after it had finally dawned on her that Brady was matchmaking.

It was so blatant, so obvious, so glaring, she still couldn't imagine how she'd missed it before.

But somehow she had. Oh, she'd known all along that he and Nick and Mikey really liked her. The feeling was mutual. And she'd known from the long talks she'd had with the boys during Mrs. Kiltz's regime that all three were tired of baby-sitters and unhappy about Alex's frequent absences. And hadn't she suspected it was more than coincidence that every time they needed her for something, she and Alex wound up face to face?

Yes. So why had it taken her so long to put the pieces together?

Could it be, she'd asked herself as she'd watched the moon blaze a silver path across the Sound last night, that on some level she'd known all along what was going on but had chosen to ignore it? Because deep down inside, she'd recognized that if she acknowledged the boys' hopes, she'd have to examine her own?

Yes. Finally, there'd been no avoiding the truth. Just as there'd been no more ignoring the questions she'd been dodging for the past several weeks.

What did she want from Alex? What did she want for him? And what did she want for herself?

Of the three, the second question was the easiest. She wanted Alex to have the kind of relationship with his sons that she hadn't had with her own parents. No longer just because the boys needed him. But because, with every encounter, she'd come to see how much *he* needed them. They were as good for him as he was for them, and lately, that had started to matter. A lot.

What she wanted *from* Alex was more difficult. While their polite camaraderie was okay, it wasn't enough, since it didn't address her undeniable physical attraction to him. To her chagrin, while *he* seemed perfectly in control, she was wrestling a desire to touch him that was growing stronger with each encounter, each conversation, each problem they faced together.

She wanted him. Which, she acknowledged with a chagrined groan, pretty much answered question number three.

Except that the little voice in her head had refused to let her off so easy. *Come on, Skipper,* it had said. *Don't stop being honest now. This is just getting interesting. Go ahead. Admit it. You want Alex to quit seeing you merely as the boys' friend and start seeing you as a woman.*

A woman who interested him not just as a sex object—although that wouldn't hurt for a start—but as a person. A person who could get past that wall of reserve he erected whenever things started to get interesting.

Of course, there was about as much chance of that happening as there was of Brady suddenly developing a mad passion for ballet, Shay thought now, in the clear light of morning.

People were what they were, and felt what they felt. Clearly, despite that single kiss they'd shared, her feelings for Alex were one-sided, and the vague hopes she'd been harboring that something might develop between them were preposterous.

She shook her head at her own foolishness. Hadn't her upbringing taught her that the only person you could count on to look out for your needs was yourself? Hadn't she learned at an early age that she was responsible for her own happiness? Didn't she know by now that life was too short to wait for somebody else to fulfill her?

Yes. Absolutely. Which was why it was time she quit lying awake nights thinking about Alex and waiting for something to happen that wasn't going to. It was time to get back to concentrating on her future.

The phone sounded again. Yawning, she sat up and shoved her hair out of her face. "Hold on. I'm coming," she murmured. She ignored the steps that led up to the end of the raised bed and half rolled, half fell off the side to the floor four feet below. She yanked down the hem of her thigh-high sleep shirt and slogged over to the phone. "'Lo?"

"Shay?"

She squinted across the room at the digital clock on the VCR. "It's ten to seven, Brady." She really needed a cup of coffee.

"I know, but—can you come over here?"

Buoyed with newfound resolution, she said firmly, "No. I can't. This time you've gone too far, kiddo—"

"But you have to!"

She straightened as she realized the boy's voice sounded funny. Muffled. Breathless. Agitated. "What's the matter? There isn't something wrong with Mikey's new goldfish, is there?"

"No, it's Daddy! You've got to come! Right away!"

"Brady—"

"Please, Shay? I can't wake him up!"

Her heart stopped. "Oh, my—Brady, listen to me. Call 911, sweetie, and then go down and unlock the front door for me, okay? I'll be right there."

She dropped the phone and looked wildly around. Spying her running shoes, she jammed her feet into them. Then she tore open her door and dashed across the front lawn, across the asphalt drive and onto the path that linked the two dwellings, barely aware of the pale sunshine sifting through the tree leaves.

She tried to imagine what could've happened. Could it be a heart attack? A stroke? She sucked in her breath, struck by a wave of guilt. Because of Alex's killer physique, his relative youth, she'd just assumed he was as healthy as he looked.

But what did she know about him—really? He could have any number of hidden health problems. High blood pressure. A heart murmur. Diabetes. A brain tumor.

Oh, Lord. If only she hadn't tricked him into taking on the boys! If he died, they'd be orphans. And it would be all her fault!

Running hard, she popped out of the woods onto the lawn and headed toward the front door, which was wide open. Without shortening her stride, she sailed inside and on up the stairs, her feet barely touching the risers in her haste.

She sprinted along the balcony, past the children's wing. She wondered where Brady was. On the phone with 911? She started to call out, but stopped herself when she realized she didn't know if the other boys were awake or not. For a fleeting second it occurred to her to wonder why he'd been trying to wake Alex at such an early hour in the first place. Then she forgot everything as she reached her destination.

She stopped, poised on the threshold of Alex's silent, shadow-filled room. Heavy dark curtains stretched across the wall to her left, hiding the French doors that opened onto the balcony. To her right were the doors that led to the walk-in closet and the bathroom. Sunshine spilled from the latter's skylight.

The bed was right in front of her. It was wide and low, covered with a navy blue silk spread. A big, still shape was sprawled in the middle of it.

Please, God, don't let him be dead.

She took a deep breath and tiptoed over.

Alex lay faceup, arms outstretched, the covers bunched at his waist. As she'd already had occasion to see, his chest was wide and well-defined. A soft whorl of dark curls stretched from nipple to nipple, then narrowed into a thinner line that bisected his flat belly and disappeared under the covers.

His shoulders and torso lifted slightly. A wave of relief rolled over her; he was breathing.

Which didn't mean anything. He could be unconscious. He could be in a coma. *He could die of old age if you don't take action and quit acting so silly.*

Yet she couldn't help but note that he looked different in repose. Younger. Less intimidating. More approachable. His gold-streaked hair was tumbled over his brow, his cheeks shadowed with a faint smudge of beard. Yet there was a clean strength to the angle of his jaw, to his lean cheeks and straight nose, that made him look strong and capable even now. He had the kind of face that would age well.

If he doesn't expire while you stand here gawking.

All right, all right. She leaned over and gingerly laid her palm against one strong shoulder. "Alex?" she whispered. His skin was warm and smooth, like sun-warmed satin. Touching him made a tingle start up her arm. It turned into a shiver that ran down her spine before an all-over ache bloomed to life.

She forced herself to ignore it. She gave him a little shake. "Alex?"

One corner of his mouth lifted in a crooked smile. "Shay?" he murmured huskily.

Her heart jumped. It was because he was coming around, she told herself firmly. Not because of the way he'd said her name. She tugged on his shoulder again. "Wake up, Alex. Please."

For a second nothing happened. And then his eyes snapped open and he stared at her in utter astonishment. With a startled cry, he rocketed upright, clutching the covers to his chin. "What the hell! What are you doing here!" he yelled.

Shay recoiled with a shriek of her own.

"Surprise!" the boys yelled from the doorway.

Grinning like pint-size loons, they trotted into the room and advanced on the pair of distraught adults. "We made you breakfast in bed," Brady said, chortling, oblivious to the intense tension gripping the room. An overloaded tray wobbled precariously in his hands.

"For our two most favoritest grown-ups in the whole, wide world," Nick said proudly.

"'Cuz Daddy's our daddy and Shay's our fwiend," Mikey contributed shyly.

"I bet you're really surprised, aren't you?" Nick said with a chuckle. "I bet you never guessed in a zillion years we'd do something so cool."

"Yeah," Brady agreed happily. "But we did. So now we can all be together—" he plopped the tray down on the bed "—just like a real family."

Alex stared at Brady. His face turned slightly purple, making Shay fear he might have an actual coronary. He shook his head. "I can't—I don't—" He ground to a halt, too overcome to say another word.

"That's okay, Daddy," Brady said. Beaming at Alex, he reached out and patted his father's blanket-covered knee. "You don't have to thank us. Neat stuff like this is what kids are for."

Eight

"**D**oes everybody understand the rules?" Alex popped the action-adventure movie into the VCR and scrutinized his sons. The trio was spread out before the TV set, Nick sprawled on the couch, Brady draped sideways in a chair, Mikey lying on the floor.

Brady rolled his eyes. "Yes, Daddy."

"Well, let's go over them one more time just to be sure."

The two older boys groaned. Before Alex could say another word, they chanted, "'We're supposed to sit here and watch the movie. We aren't supposed to touch anything except the remote control. We're not supposed to leave the room, except to go to the bathroom. We're not supposed to turn anything on, take anything apart or do anything to Mikey. In an hour you'll take a break from your work and fix us root beer floats.'"

Alex nodded in approval. "You've got it."

Brady sighed, his expression sulky. "I don't want to watch this dumb old movie. It's boring. I want to go outside."

"Yeah," Nick whined. "Why can't we go outside?"

Alex glanced out the window. The afternoon was gray, grim and damp. "Because it's raining."

"But we like to play in the rain," Brady said peevishly.

"Yeah. We never get to do anything," Nick complained.

Alex stared at him in disbelief. The kid is tired, he reminded himself. They were *all* tired, and with good cause.

Alex had reached his limit yesterday during that incredible breakfast-in-bed caper. There he'd been, angry, frustrated and self-conscious, when it had dawned on him that what he really, really wanted to do—even more than throttle his sons—was to toss them out of the room and toss *Shay* onto the bed. He'd been so disturbed by the desire—and the suspicion that the lady in question was stark naked under her skimpy sleep shirt—he'd eaten an entire piece of peanut butter toast before it dawned on him the little sprinkles on it weren't sprinkles at all. That the boys had dropped it on the way upstairs and the sprinkles he'd consumed were...rug fuzz.

Something inside him had snapped. He'd come off the bed like a tiger, hustled Shay out of the house and read the boys the riot act. Then, after weighing the potential harm of sending them the wrong signal against the peril of running into Shay again, he'd showered, loaded the terrible trio into the car and gone to Seattle, where they'd spent the day at the waterfront.

They'd ridden the trolley, fed sea gulls, watched the ferries dock and depart, visited the Aquarium and taken in the Omnidome laser show.

It should have been fun. It should have been educational. It should have been memorable.

Instead, Alex had been tense and the boys disgruntled. Every other word out of their mouths had been *Shay*. "I bet Shay would like this." "Shay told me a story once..." "If Shay was here..." "Shay says..."

The worst of it was, Alex had missed her himself. Not, he was quick to assure himself, because he couldn't handle

things or because he'd started to depend on her or anything.

But because he knew she would have enjoyed it. She
would have chuckled at the seals' antics and enjoyed feed-
ing sea gulls. Her big dark eyes would have widened at the
laser show, warmed at the boys' glee at ringing the trolley
bell and gleamed with suppressed laughter when the sea cu-
cumber spat on Brady.

And somehow, when Shay was having fun, the day
seemed a little brighter and the world a little better.

"Gee, Daddy." Brady windmilled his arms restlessly. "I
still don't see why we can't go outside."

"Because I said so," Alex said flatly. "I have to go over
the monthly reports from my managers and that's all there
is to it. You guys are just going to have to manage." With
that he flipped on the movie, walked out of the room and
down the hall to his study. Careful to leave the door open—
he was learning—he sat down at his desk, turned on the
computer and got down to work.

He'd just switched on the printer some forty-five minutes later when the doorbell rang. He waited a minute to see
that his reports were printing correctly, then went and
opened the front door.

"Hi." Shay stood on the porch. Raindrops sparkled in
her inky hair, and her creamy skin was flushed. She had on
tennis shoes, itty-bitty running shorts and a tank top under
a zip-front sweatshirt.

Didn't the woman own any *real* clothes? "Hi."

"Am I interrupting?" She smiled uncertainly.

"No, of course not." And was there some specific reason why her teeth had to be so even and white, her mouth so
unbearably exotic? "What can I do for you?"

"Do you have a minute? I'd like to talk to you."

"Sure. Come on in." He stepped back, waited for her to
enter and shut the door.

"Thanks."

A sound came from the back of the house. He frowned. "Excuse me. Just let me check this out, okay?" He started down the hall, the back of his neck tingling as she followed along. He pushed open the swinging door to the kitchen, speaking over his shoulder. "The boys are in the family room—"

Only they weren't. They were in the kitchen, swirling around the room like human tornadoes. "It's been an hour!" Nick said quickly when he saw Alex.

"Yeah!" Brady agreed. He opened the freezer and tossed a container of ice cream to Mikey, then reached into the fridge and snagged the milk and a bottle of root beer. Leaving both compartment doors ajar, he scurried over to the counter, dragged the blender close and dumped in ingredients with the blinding speed of a mad scientist. "We want root beer milkshakes but you don't have to worry 'cuz we can do it ourselves."

"Now wait one darn second—"

"We want popcorn, too, okay?" On the opposite side of the room, Nick stuffed a bag into the microwave.

"Hey! It's Shay!" Mikey said happily, spying her at Alex's shoulder.

Nick's face lit up. "Hi! Guess what? I've got a rash. Want to see?"

"It's disgusting," Brady warned her. "I bet you'd like the movie though. It's really cool! Want to watch with us?"

"I don't think so, guys. I came to talk to your dad."

"Please?"

She laughed, shaking her head; the sound scraped against Alex's raw nerves, drawing his attention away from the boys for what proved to be one fateful second.

Nick hit the microwave On button, Brady punched the blender's Pulverize switch and the refrigerator cycled on— all at the same time. There was a moment of ear-splitting din.

The lights blinked out. The appliances died with a pitiful whine.

"Well, heck," Alex said. On top of everything else, now he had an electrical problem.

"It sure is dark down here," Shay said, as she and Alex descended the basement stairway.

"What did you expect? I told you the basement and the kitchen are on the same circuit. That's why I've got the flashlight." He grimaced. He was being brusque to the point of rudeness and he knew it, but as usual he couldn't seem to help it.

"It was just an observation, Alex," she said mildly. "You don't have to take my head off. It wasn't my idea to come down here. I would have been happy to stay upstairs with the boys—"

"Oh, right. So you could help them clean up that mess? No way. They have to learn the consequences of their actions."

"Yes, they do. But they *are* just little kids. Anyone can leave the top off a blender. I've done it myself. Don't you think you were a little hard on them?"

"No, I do not."

She was silent a moment. "Alex?"

"What?"

"You're not still peeved because I lent you that money at the grocery store, are you?"

"I was not peeved."

"Or vexed about what I said about your underwear? Because I really didn't mean it the way it sounded—"

"Forget it."

"Are you irritated because I intervened with Mikey's fish, then?"

"Don't be ridiculous."

"Okay. Then what's the problem?"

A muscle twitched in his jaw. The problem was that she was too close and it was too damn dark. A man could get dangerous ideas. He could start thinking of all the things he'd like to do. With her. To her. And what she could do to him if she were of a mind to....

"Well?"

"Look," he snapped. "You said you wanted to talk to me, so why don't you just get to it?"

Shay shook her head. He really was sexy. His burgundy polo shirt hugged his broad shoulders, his fanny was perfect for his soft oyster-colored cords, and he smelled like a dream.

It was too bad he was always so crabby. It made it difficult to speak openly. But maybe, if she eased into it... "This isn't the first time I've tried to talk to you, you know. I came by yesterday, but you weren't here." Great. Now *she* sounded crabby. Or, worse, as if she were checking up on him.

"I took the boys to Seattle. To the waterfront."

"Oh." She knew it was ridiculous, but for a second she actually felt hurt that he'd left her behind. *Grow up, Spenser.* She raised her chin and forced herself to speak pleasantly. "Did you have fun?"

"Absolutely. It was great. Terrific. Now, are you going to tell me what you wanted, or not?"

"Brady is matchmaking." There. It was out. How would he react? Would he be shocked? Appalled? Would he even believe her?

"I know."

"You do?" It was the one possibility that hadn't occurred to her.

"Uh-huh."

"Oh. When did you figure it out?"

He shrugged. "I suspected we'd been set up that day at the grocery store. I guess I knew for sure the day the sink overflowed four times. It seemed pretty obvious."

"But... why didn't you say something?"

"I didn't see a reason to. I figured we're both mature adults. Smart enough to know that just because Brady wants something to happen, doesn't mean it's going to."

"Oh. Right."

"Now, would you mind being quiet while I get my bearings?"

Shay couldn't believe it. If they hadn't already reached the foot of the stairs she would have given him a swift push down the remaining ones. She had to settle instead for glaring at the back of his head as he headed toward the farthest, darkest corner of the basement.

She stuck to him like glue. The room was huge, half the size of the house. In addition to the laundry facilities, it also housed the heating and air-conditioning systems and a giant-size hot water tank. Tools, furniture and other seasonal items loomed, big and black in the inky gloom. Pipes pinged, air ducts rattled; overhead, the floor creaked and settled. Even though she knew it was silly, the place gave her the willies.

They finally came to a stop next to a jumble of boxes and miscellaneous furniture that included an old-fashioned tester bed.

"What is all this stuff?" she asked him.

He ran the flashlight beam over the wall, then gave a grunt of satisfaction as he located the breaker box. "The old bedroom furniture from the cottage," he said absently. He pulled on the front plate. "Here. Hold the torch, would you? The latch seems to be stuck."

Shay leaned forward to take it, resting her hand on a chest of drawers for balance.

Something small and furry darted across the back of her wrist.

With a strangled scream, she snatched her hand away and leapt forward, flinging herself at Alex. Their legs tangled together and they pitched sideways onto the bed, sending the flashlight flying from his hand. It arced crazily through the air. Light strobed across the ceiling, followed by a dull thud and a tinkle of glass. The room went black.

There was a moment's dead silence.

"What the hell," Alex said finally, his warm breath feathering across Shay's chest, "was that all about?"

Heat coiled through her. He was sprawled atop her, partway down her body, his torso between her shorts-clad thighs, his cheek nestled intimately between her breasts. A hollow feeling bloomed in her stomach. She couldn't seem to catch her breath. She waited, tense with anticipation, although she wasn't quite sure for what. "B-Brutus, I think. He ran up my arm."

There was another pause. "Ah. My nemesis. The Dr. Richard Kimbell of gerbils. I should've known."

Oh, dear. Had that been a glimmer of humor? She felt a thrill of alarm. Given his proximity, if he suddenly got halfway charming on her, she'd be in serious trouble.

Who are you trying to kid, Skip? You're beyond trouble. You've got both feet—not to mention the rest of you—solidly planted in the danger zone.

Or, to be more accurate... under it.

"I should've expected this," Alex went on. "I seem to be on some sort of cosmic plan, a disaster a day the minimum."

He sounded tired. Not to mention discouraged, disgruntled and a little baffled.

Her heart lurched. "But... you've been here for the boys." As if her hand had a will of its own, she reached down and gently brushed the hair off his forehead, the gesture meant to be consoling. "That's the important part."

He shuddered at her touch. "A hell of a lot of good I've done. I've screwed up everything I've tried. You know what I said about going to Seattle yesterday? About having a good time? I lied. It was awful. I lost Mikey in the Aquarium. I had to call Security, and the thirty minutes before we found him asleep by the octopus tank were the longest thirty minutes of my life. Then I let Nick eat a strawberry ice-cream cone before I remembered he's allergic to the fruit. Within an hour he was covered in welts. We had to go to the Visitors' Aid Station, which took so long my car was nearly towed. As it was, the overtime fine alone was enough to put Brady through college."

She didn't know whether to laugh or cry. "Oh, Alex—"

"I'm not done. It took twice as long to get home because an accident closed down the freeway. When we finally got here, the boys insisted on sleeping with me because of the rainstorm and I woke up this morning on the floor. So I thought I'd try to get the kinks out with some exercise, but that damn gerbil has chewed holes in all my athletic shoes."

"Oh, dear," she said with a strangled chuckle. "I'm sorry." The words seemed woefully inadequate.

"Yeah? Well, that's not the worst part."

"What is?"

"You just keep being nice. On top of everything else, I've been a rude jerk. *I'm* the one who ought to apologize."

"Oh, Alex." She cupped his cheek in her palm. She wasn't sure *what* she was doing, but she knew she wasn't trying to console him. Her thumb stroked a lazy pattern along the firm line of his jaw.

He went very still. A soft, agonized sound broke from his lips. And then he turned his head and pressed his open mouth to the erect and aching tip of her cotton-covered breast.

It was the most carnal, shocking, exciting thing she'd ever experienced.

It was exactly what she wanted.

"Oh, Alex," she said breathlessly, arching up into that sweet wet heat. "Oh, Alex, *yes."*

It was all the encouragement he needed. His hands swept up. One closed firmly over her unclaimed breast, thumbing the quivering nipple. The other cupped the straining mound beneath his lips, holding it steady as his mouth clamped down, hot, greedy and demanding.

Need exploded inside her. Whimpering, she slid her fingers into the cool silk of his hair, her heart thundering as she imagined how glorious it would feel trailing over her naked flesh. Beneath her hands, she could feel his cheeks hollow in time to the steady pull of his lips. The insistent tugging brought her bowing up off the bed.

It was almost too much. And not nearly enough.

Her grip tightened on his hair and a shudder went through him. He lifted his head. "What?" He was breathing hard, his heaving chest pressed achingly against her most intimate place. "Do you want me to stop?"

"Don't you dare," she said fiercely. "*Kiss me.*"

He made a sound low in his throat, raised himself up and moved higher. His weight slammed her down into the billowing mattress as the flat, hard angles of his body fitted into her rounded curves like a bolt sliding into a socket.

She slanted her head, crazy for the taste of him, shuddering with pleasure as his lips slid over hers. "Oh, Alex." She'd never felt like this. Hot. Wild. Utterly and completely out of control. As if she'd die if she couldn't have him.

As if she'd die if she did.

She opened her mouth for the thrust of his tongue. On fire with the need to touch him, she yanked his shirt out of his cords, savoring the way he inhaled sharply when she swept her hands up the smooth flesh of his sides. She slid her palms over the bunched heat of his chest, explored the hard muscle of his pectorals, the smooth line of his collarbone. She reached around and traced the sharp planes of his shoulder blades, then followed the strong straight valley of his spine down to the small of his back. She pulled him closer, her heart kicking into overdrive as she felt the rigid swell of his arousal pressed against her through his slacks.

He groaned and ran his hand up under her shirt.

They both moaned as his fingers spread out, swarmed over her stomach, sneaked under her bra and cradled the aching mound of her bare breast. "Damn. You feel so—"

A clatter of noise shattered the quiet. It was followed by the murmur of high, excited voices. "Hello-o-o? Daddy? Shay? We got the kitchen cleaned up. Are you guys down there?"

"Ohmigosh! It's the boys!" Shay clutched Alex for dear life. "What are we going to do?"

"Don't move," he hissed. "Maybe... maybe they'll go away."

She felt a hysterical urge to laugh. He couldn't be serious, could he?

There was a hum of sound, like a swarm of bees, as the boys consulted. Their silhouettes could be clearly seen backlit by the dull gray afternoon light that illuminated the upper landing. Shay held her breath, only to tense in disbelief when Brady suddenly said clearly, "There! I got it!"

A beam of light bloomed to life. It caromed once around the room, then cut swiftly through the darkness until it honed right in on them.

"Well, *hell.* They've got a flashlight!" Alex shot off the bed like a scalded cat, dragging Shay with him. No more than five seconds later, the light again began to move, shooting past where they now stood, before it reversed and steadied on them.

"There you are," Brady said triumphantly. Followed by Mike and Nick, he clattered most of the way down the stairs. "We thought you were lost. Did you drop your flashlight? You musta. I bet you're glad we showed up, aren'tcha?"

Alex raised a hand to shield his eyes from the blinding light. "Oh... yeah. Glad."

His voice sounded hoarse and wheezy, as if he'd been engaged in something strenuous. Or scandalous, Shay thought with a blush. Lord knew, she felt hot and achy. Not only that, but her knees didn't want to work. The only thing keeping her on her feet was the iron grip of Alex's arm around her waist.

She'd never felt so stripped down to the bare essentials and exposed in her life.

But it wasn't almost being caught by the boys in flagrante delicto that was the cause of those feelings.

It was the realization that her earlier thought had been one hundred percent true.

She'd never felt like this. Hot. Wild. Utterly and completely out of control. As if she'd die if she couldn't have a man. As if she'd die if she couldn't have . . . Alex.

Good grief. Now she knew why she couldn't stay away. She loved him.

The minute the thought entered her head, she tried to deny it. This wasn't love, she told herself firmly. It was just excess attraction.

"You know," Nick said thoughtfully. "You guys look kind of funny. Your hair is all stick-uppy."

"Yep. He's right," Brady concurred happily. "Your clothes look messy, too."

Shay glanced down. Sure enough, her sweatshirt was hanging off one shoulder, her tank top was untucked, one sock was half off and she was actually missing a tennis shoe. Yet it was nothing compared to her emotional disarray.

"Great," Alex murmured in disgust. "The same kids who like to put their underwear on their heads and dance around the room have to choose *now* to develop fashion sense."

"What were you guys doing?" Brady asked in a gleeful voice that suggested he already knew.

Nick gave a snort of disgust. "Gee, Brady, didn't you see? It was that mushy disgusting stuff, like those people on that TV show Mrs. Kiltz liked to watch. You know—'The Young and the Wrestlers'?"

"We were doing no such thing," Alex said firmly. "We were looking for our flashlight."

Shay raised her chin. "That's right."

"I don't think so," Brady said gleefully. "I think—"

"Wow, look!" Nick drowned him out, his voice rising in excitement. "It's Brutus!"

"Where?" Mikey cried.

"Right there!" Nick said.

"I see him!" Brady crowed.

"Where?" Mikey repeated.

"There!" Nick bellowed. "Get him! Get him!"

There was a thud as the flashlight dropped and rolled down the remaining stairs, then the sound of a scuffle as all three boys presumably tried to chase after the fleeing gerbil at once.

"Hey! Watch it!" came Brady's alarmed voice. It was followed by a startled "Eyooow!" and a sound like a bowling ball thumping down the stairs.

Then there was silence.

Nine

"**I** should have taken him into Seattle for a C.A.T. scan," Alex said, glancing at Shay as he finally gave voice to the thought that had been dogging him for hours. They were headed downstairs after tucking Brady in for the umpteenth time that night.

"Alex, he's fine," she said firmly. "No one has ever died from a bruise on the shin. Although, knowing Brady, and given the amount of attention this is getting him, he may be bedridden for months."

In just the past hour alone, the eight-year-old had kept both of them hopping. He'd needed his sheets smoothed, a drink of water, a dose of children's pain reliever, an extra pillow for his leg, a back rub, a lighter weight blanket, a neck massage and his favorite bedtime story read twice.

Rationally, Alex knew she was right. Yet for some strange reason, he couldn't seem to stop worrying. "Maybe Dr. Richter missed something," he theorized.

"*No*. He took X rays, remember? Not once. Not twice. But three times. From every conceivable angle. You looked at them. I looked at them. The *janitor* looked at them. If he's in danger from anything, it's radiation poisoning. The residents of Chernobyl were exposed to fewer gamma rays than Brady got today. If there was a problem, the doctor would have found it."

He ran a hand through his hair, feeling suddenly sheepish. "You're right. I'm overreacting. I don't know what's wrong with me."

"Maybe it's hormone overload," she offered helpfully. "Adrenaline is great when you need it, but when it wears off, it leaves you wrung out."

He looked at her, taking in her tousled hair, her flushed cheeks, her slim legs in her little shorts, and was suddenly conscious of a familiar ache beating through him. "I don't think that's it," he murmured. Although she might have a point about the hormone thing, he was pretty sure it was testosterone, not adrenaline, that was affecting him.

"Well, then," she said as they reached the foyer, "maybe you're just tired. It has been a long day. And you said earlier that you didn't get much rest last night. A good night's sleep is probably the answer."

Again, he didn't think so. Not now that he knew exactly how soft and silky and delicious she was beneath the casual cover of her shorts and shirt. And how satiny her nipples felt against his palms, and the way her breath caught in her throat when he nipped the plush cushion of her lower lip.

He stifled a groan. Who was he kidding? He didn't have a tinker's chance in hell of sleeping a wink—not if he had to go to bed alone.

He was *still* trying to figure out what had happened between them earlier in the basement. Not the sex part—it was pretty damn clear that the attraction between them was hot and getting hotter. Not that you'd know it at the moment, however, given the way she was edging for the door. She sure wasn't giving any sign that she wanted to pick up where they'd left off...dammit.

No, it was what had occurred before their earlier passionate interlude, when he'd found himself confessing his feelings and sharing his insecurities, that was *really* disturbing. And what had happened afterward, when he'd found he was relying on her strength and good judgment to see him through the crisis with Brady. Why, the last time he could recall feeling so at ease, so close to anyone, had been four years ago. When Ali was still alive....

Shay glanced at her watch. "I really should get going so you can get some rest," she said, taking a backward step toward the door.

"No," he said without thinking. Whatever the cause, he felt restless, on edge, and nowhere near ready to give up her company.

She stared at him in surprise. "What?"

"I'll walk you home." Was it his imagination, or did she actually look dismayed for a second.

"That's all right. You don't need to—"

He cut her off. "I could use some fresh air. And exercise. Besides, finding Mrs. Rosencrantz here when we got back from the doctor's office was one of the few *good* surprises I've had in two weeks. I'm sure she won't mind being asked to listen for the boys." She shouldn't—not after he'd given her a fifteen percent raise, offered to hire a cleaning crew and have the laundry sent out from now on, if only she wouldn't quit when she got a good look at the kitchen. "Let me go talk to her and I'll be right back." He strode away before Shay could protest further.

As he'd surmised, the housekeeper was feeling pretty mellow about the sudden positive turn in her fortunes. She was more than happy to hold down the fort. She even told him to take his time.

He found Shay waiting outside. "We're all set," he told her. He paused to allow his eyes to adjust, then followed her down the steps and across the lawn. The night was balmy.

A light but steady breeze had cleared the clouds away, making way for a three-quarter moon and a scattering of stars. The sweet smell of rain-washed grass and flowers perfumed the air. The solar-powered landscape lights that twinkled at the edge of the drive and along the various paths gave the grounds a festive air.

Shay tried to concentrate on the soft rustle of the breeze through the trees and the occasional chirrup of frogs and crickets, but it was hopeless. All she could think about was Alex—and she wasn't doing that too clearly.

Any last vestige of doubt she'd had about how much he cared for his kids had been obliterated in the past few hours. She'd seen the utter terror he couldn't hide before they'd known for sure Brady was all right. She'd seen the effort he'd made to get his fears under control for the children's sake. And she'd seen his vulnerable side when he'd shared his worries.

Needless to say, it had only added to her regard for him, strengthening the startling idea she'd had earlier that she'd tried to deny. She loved him.

Way to go, Skip, said her little voice. *Leave it to you to do the one thing most guaranteed to complicate your life.*

He cleared his throat. "I don't think I thanked you."

"For what?"

"For sticking around and helping when Brady fell. For being so calm and unshakable. You're pretty good in a crisis."

"I've had some practice." She relaxed at the neutral subject. At least he didn't seem aware of her feelings.

He was silent a moment. "Do you miss it?"

"What?"

"Your job. The danger and excitement. Being at the center of the action."

"It hasn't exactly been dull around here the past few weeks," she pointed out.

"You know what I mean."

She sobered. "Yes, I do. And the answer is no. I loved what I was doing while I was doing it, but there was always something missing—I just didn't want to admit it."

"So what changed?"

"I won that darned Pulitzer."

"That was bad?"

She laughed softly. "No, that was good. But it made me take a good, long look at what I was doing, how I was living my life. I started to realize some things—and they didn't make me happy."

"Like?"

"Well, I began to see I was doing what my parents had done, pouring everything into my job. And that my relationships were all work related, which was hardly surprising, since the kind of life I'd been leading—always on the road, living out of a suitcase, following a story at the drop of a hat—wasn't exactly conducive to a personal life. It sounds corny, but I woke up one morning and realized I wasn't burned out so much as I was just plain tired of having no roots, of always feeling alone."

Alex nodded. Her admission struck a chord. Without making a conscious decision, he heard himself say, "After Allison died, once the worst of the grief had passed, it was the loneliness that was hardest to take." He shook his head. "All the intimate things I'd come to take for granted over the years—having someone special to share a joke with or scratch the spot in the middle of my back or who knew I liked to sleep on the left side of the bed— it was all gone in an instant."

"It must've been hard," she said quietly.

"Did Beau tell you what happened?"

"He mentioned an aneurysm."

He sighed. "She put the boys down for their naps one afternoon when Mikey was six months old, lay down herself and never got up. I came home early from work and there she was. She'd suffered a brain hemorrhage in her sleep."

She could picture it. Too clearly. "I'm sorry." She reached out and clasped his hand in hers, offering belated comfort.

He stared blindly down at their linked fingers. "She'd been complaining off and on of a headache for days. I told her to go to the doctor, but she didn't. We'd just closed the deal on our second resort and money was tight—we were still paying for Mikey's birth, and Ali was always trying to economize." He sighed. "It was as if one minute I had this perfect life. And the next, I didn't have anything."

Shay squeezed his hand. "I'm sorry," she said again.

Before she could say anything more, he said quietly, in a tone of voice that made it clear he'd prefer they drop the subject, "Four years is a long time. It's in the past."

He didn't speak again until they reached the cottage.

"Well, good night," she said lightly, turning to face him. "And thanks for the escort. It's been . . . interesting."

"Shay—" He hesitated, clearly uneasy. "About what happened earlier in the basement... I don't usually come on to women that way. I'm not sure what happened."

"It's all right." The last thing she wanted was an apology for something she'd found so wonderful.

"No, it's not." The breeze blew a strand of hair across her cheek. He reached out and gently pushed it behind her ear. "One minute we were talking and then, I don't know. I got carried away and lost control and—"

"Alex, please." She pressed a finger to his lips, trying to stem the flow of words. "It's never been that way for me before, either."

He reached up and gently captured her hand, sliding it sideways and holding it against the side of his face. "What do you mean?"

"I've never felt that way. That needful. That . . . ardent. I've never wanted anyone the way I wanted you."

It was as if her honest admission had knocked the props out from underneath him. "You haven't?" His voice was raw with disbelief.

"No."

There was a weighty silence. He sighed. "Damn. I wish you hadn't said that." He tugged her close, tangled his hands in the inky satin of her hair and tipped her face up to his. He lowered his head.

His mouth found hers unerringly. Just as before, they fitted as if made for each other. There was no awkward fumbling, no bumping noses, no tentative touches. Just that overwhelming sense of rightness as they kissed, hot and hungry. His mouth canted against hers, his tongue delved inside, stroking her sleek inner reaches.

Shay moaned, overcome with delicious sensation. With every touch, she wanted more. His lips were warm and firm, his body hot and hard. She linked her hands around his neck, taking delight in the rasp of his slightly whiskered chin against her cheek, the slight tremor of his fingers as he cradled her skull, the firm press of his chest against her tender breasts.

By the time they came up for air, they were both quivering like a pair of engines cranked to full throttle.

"Damn." Alex gave a shaky laugh and leaned his forehead against hers. "I haven't felt like this since Sarah Jane Fenster let me kiss her behind the bleachers in high school."

"Lucky Sarah." Standing in the V of his thighs, she could feel the thick ridge of his arousal pressing against her. She sighed tremulously. "*Nobody* felt like this—" she nudged her hips against his "—when I was in school."

He groaned. "Shay—"

"*Alex—*" she mimicked his scolding tone perfectly. When he gave a hoarse chuckle, she turned her head and pressed a kiss to his mouth. "That's so nice," she whispered.

"What?" His hands stroked down her back.

"Hearing you laugh." Throwing caution to the wind, she slid her lips across his cheek to taste the silky patch of skin behind his ear with her tongue.

He shuddered. "Shay—"

"Shhh. Please, Alex. I want you...."

Those three little words, uttered in her throaty voice, were all it took. He swept her into his arms and shouldered aside the door, kicking it shut as he carried her inside.

The interior of the cottage was filled with moonlight. Reflected by the Sound, it poured through the expanse of glass that formed the back wall, glittering and waving against the walls with the water's every surge and swell.

Grateful for the illumination, Alex strode toward the bed, his mouth fused to Shay's. He paused when he reached the raised platform. "Leave it to Beau to complicate matters," he muttered, tossing her gently onto the high, wide mattress. He kicked off his shoes and vaulted after her. "Why the hell can't he have a normal bed like normal people...?"

She laughed. The deep, breathy sound set his nerves ajangle as they rolled across the spacious expanse, shedding clothes every which way.

When they came to a stop, they were both naked—and Alex was on top. Shay's laughter died as she looked up and saw his expression. Passion had done what nothing else could, stripping away his elegant, civilized facade.

"I'll try to go slow," he said hoarsely, his eyes shadowed as he looked down at her. He rocked back onto his knees, his chest and shoulders rigid, his expression strained as he tried to check the desire riding him. "But I'm not making any promises. Not the first time, anyway. After that, we'll see...."

He trailed his fingers up the inside of her thighs, bent forward, dipped his head and brushed a butterfly kiss to her navel. His mouth was hot, magical, bold. He began to string a necklace of kisses across her belly, leaving a chain of fire in his wake. Shay caught her breath as his hands skated higher and his thumbs deftly parted the tangle of curls that crowned her desire. He touched her, stroking with a soft, sure caress that turned her joints to jelly. A tremor went through him as he registered the slippery heat that proclaimed her need was as great as his.

Her hips rose to meet his touch. She didn't know how he could mistake what she wanted, but just to make sure he understood, she said his name. "Alex?"

"What?"

"Forget slow. *Hurry.*"

"Hell." He slid his hands up her torso and braced himself above her. He bent his golden head and pressed a damp kiss to the beaded tip of her nipple, then slid his lips higher, forging a trail across the delicate curve of her collarbone and up the slender column of her neck. With a hunger that would have been frightening if it hadn't perfectly matched her own, he settled his mouth over hers, taking her with a kiss that was deep and demanding, a taste of things to come.

His arousal nudged her. She whimpered and he lifted his head. His gaze was fierce in the silvery night. "Are you sure?" he asked hoarsely.

She reached up, thrust her shaking fingers into his hair and yanked his mouth back down to hers. "Are you crazy? Yes." She raked her teeth across his bottom lip for good measure.

He flexed his hips and she cried out with satisfaction at that first sweet, incredible pressure. He flexed again and slid fully home, filling her with pleasure. "Oh. *Yes.*" With that raspy sigh of affirmation, she wrapped her legs around the backs of his thighs and arched up to bring him even deeper.

Alex drew back as far as he could and moved again, gritting his teeth against the need that crowded him. She was making him crazy. Every soft little cry was like a lash, driving him closer to the climax he was determined to hold off. "Dammit," he gasped. "I want this to be good for you."

"If it gets any better," she panted, "I'll probably have a heart attack."

That did it. With a giant shudder, he gave up the battle for control and let himself go. Faster. Harder. Deeper. His heart thundered as she rose to meet every thrust. She was his perfect other half, her rhythm the consummate counterpoint for his. She matched him breath for breath, heartbeat for heartbeat, heart to heart, each rise of her slim silken body forging them together even as they slid apart.

Suddenly her fingers bit into his shoulders. Her muscles clenched, and the soft glove of her body tightened around him. He felt a rush of heat race along her velvet skin before she arched even higher beneath him and cried out. Her voice was rich and dark and just for him as wave after wave of release crashed through her.

Her pleasure ignited his. With a deep cry he rose up, crushed her against him and thrust again, holding the stroke as his own climax tore through him. It started so deep and lasted so long his entire body shook uncontrollably.

When it was over he collapsed, too weak to bear his own weight. He rolled to his side, his mind blank, cradling Shay against him. He was too sated, too exhausted, too stunned by the sheer unparalleled pleasure he'd just experienced to speak. Apparently so was she, because for the longest time she just lay there, plastered to his side.

Eventually, however, she reached up, cupped his cheek in her hand and drew his head down for the press of her lips. "That was...nice."

"Nice, hell," he rasped. "That was incredible." He dragged her closer and traced a circle on the downy skin of her hip. The slight movement was all he could manage; the way he felt at the moment, it might very well be all he could manage for a long, long time.

Or so he thought, until she reached down and sketched a circle of her own on the most intimate part of him, provoking an immediate—and not inconsiderable—reaction. "So. How soon before we get to try slow?"

Apparently a whole lot sooner than *he'd* thought.

Shay lay in the crook of Alex's arm, idly sifting her fingers through his thick, silky hair. She gazed blankly at the moonlight undulating on the ceiling overhead, her focus turned inward.

Any fleeting thought she may have had about the depth, the breadth, the extent of her feelings for him was gone. It had been burned away in the hours of discovery, in a journey of incredible intimacy, in the fierce and tender voyage they'd shared.

In the past few hours, she'd learned that slow and fast were definitely different but equally wonderful. She'd learned that world-class sex had no rules, just an endless array of possibilities. Most important of all, she'd learned that making love with someone you loved was an act of joy beyond anything she'd ever imagined, much less experienced.

And yet there had been no declarations of love. No exchange of endearments, no talk of the future, no promises, no commitments, no guarantees.

And it didn't matter. It didn't change a thing. Spoken or unspoken, acknowledged or not, she'd given her heart to Alex and there was no taking it back.

She didn't kid herself, however. She knew she hadn't chosen an easy path. Even though she was starting to believe Alex and his sons were the elusive, special something that would make her life complete, that didn't mean he felt the same way.

She frowned, recalling the conversation they'd had on the walk over, when he'd spoken about losing his wife. Although she wasn't proud of it—as a journalist, she was trained to consider facts, not jump to conclusions—she now realized she'd assumed he was like her parents before she'd ever met him. She'd considered him through the filter of her own experience and concluded the reason he was never home was because he valued his work over his kids.

Now she knew that wasn't true. Because now she knew that for all his presumed detachment, he hadn't ignored the boys' existence or been indifferent to their welfare or uncaring of their feelings the way her parents had hers. He never would have been so quick to take over their care the way he had if that were the case.

And now she'd heard him say in his own words how he'd felt about his wife's death.

One minute I...had a perfect life. And then I didn't have anything.

Then, she hadn't been sure what to think. But now... Now, his behavior made a terrible sort of sense. If losing his wife had hurt that much, wasn't it possible that in order to guard his heart against similar pain, he'd put everyone— including his own sons—at arm's length?

It certainly seemed likely. And if that were true, what were the chances that he'd suddenly change, suddenly tear down the barriers around his heart just because she'd fallen in love with him?

How does slim-to-none strike you, Skip?

Shay sighed. If she had an ounce of self-preservation, she'd end this now, before it went any further. She'd cut her losses and say goodbye. It would be the safest, most prudent thing to do.

And yet, she already knew she wasn't going to do it. When had she ever shied away from a challenge? Or put her personal safety above seeking out the truth? How could she walk away before she knew for sure what was possible between her and Alex?

The answer, she thought wryly, was simple.

She couldn't. One way or the other, she intended to see this through.

Beside her, Alex shifted. "Shay?" He brought his hand up and cupped her breast. "You awake?"

She turned, searching his face for some sign of his feelings for her. In the dim light the emotion in his golden eyes was impossible to gauge. Yet that didn't do a thing to dim the wave of tenderness that moved through her. Or her sudden conviction that he needed her.

Suddenly she knew that whatever the emotional risk, whatever the price she had to pay for this intimacy, this time, this pleasure, would be worth it.

Because it was Alex. Because she loved him.

A soft smile lit her face. "If I hadn't been before, I would be now," she said huskily.

She melted against him, raising her face for his kiss.

His mouth claimed hers, hot and possessive.

For now, it was more than enough.

Ten

"Look at that one," Nick crowed. "It looks like Belly!"

Shay squinted in the direction the six-year-old indicated. "Oh, I see it. You're right, Nick. It does look like a bat."

Crowded onto a double-size air mattress, she and the three boys lay on their backs in the middle of the pool, scanning the fat white clouds drifting past high overhead for familiar shapes.

The nice weather had returned, golden and hot, and the quartet had spent the afternoon enjoying it. They'd flown kites on the bluff above the Sound, had a picnic lunch in the tree house and spent the past few hours playing in the pool.

"Where's the Belly cloud?" Mikey asked anxiously. "I don't see it."

"Right there, sweetie." Careful not to swamp them, Shay reached over, turned the child's head in the correct direction and pointed. "See?"

He frowned in concentration and then his eyes widened. "Yeah! I see!" He grinned. "I wish Daddy was here so he could see it."

So did she. Alex's absence was the only dark spot in the day. Freed from having to worry about the house and meals by Mrs. Rosencrantz's return, he'd devoted the days since Brady's accident to his sons and Shay. They'd played softball and Candyland, gone sailing and swimming, had a barbecue, taken in a movie and made a day trip on the ferry to Canada. Today, however, there'd been some sort of problem with the Carstairs deal, and he'd gone into the office for a few hours to try and straighten it out.

She glanced at the cabana clock which read a quarter to five. "He should be here soon."

"Good," Nick said decisively. "'Cuz I want him to see me do that really cool cannonball you showed me."

"Well, I want him to look at clouds," Mikey said. "See that one?" He pointed at a formless blob to the left of the Belly cloud. "It looks like a pizza."

Nick gave a superior snort. "Does not."

"Does, too," Mikey said staunchly.

Hoping to head off a squabble, Shay said, "I'm sure thirsty. How about you?"

"Yeah," Nick said. "I'm really, *really* thirsty."

"Me, too," Mikey said.

"Can we have a cola?" Nick asked, looking hopeful.

"No—but you can have lemonade."

"Oh, boy!" It was their favorite, after soda pop. Without further ado, both boys jumped off the craft, which was in the shallow end, dog-paddled the few feet to the steps and climbed out.

"Don't run," Shay called after them as they started to dash toward the cabana.

They slowed to a trot. "'Kay."

Smiling, she shifted her gaze to Brady, who was lying on her other side. She shook her head as she studied him. Arms crossed behind his head, his eyes shut, he was the picture of satisfaction as he lay on his back, grinning. He'd been quieter than normal the past few days. She would have been worried if he hadn't seemed so happy.

She settled back and nudged him. "How are you?"

He opened his eyes and beamed at her. "Great." A warm gust of wind caught the mattress and pushed it toward the center of the pool. He scooted a little closer, clearly enjoying the free ride. "Shay?"

"Hmm?"

"I was wondering. Do you think I'm gonna have a scar on my leg?"

Oh, brother. "Gee, Brady, I don't think so. The last time I checked, you had to have a wound to manage that." Even though his accident was days in the past, and all he had to show for it was a faint bruise the size of a quarter, he was still milking the minor injury for all it was worth.

"Oh. I guess that means I'm not going to need an operation, doesn't it?"

"Yes, I would say so." She glanced down at him. "Is there some reason you want one?"

He slipped his hand into hers. "Well, on TV, kids always get to eat lots of ice cream."

She swallowed a bubble of laughter. "You've been watching 'The Brady Bunch' on cable again, haven't you?" For obvious reasons, he was fond of the program.

"Yeah."

"Well, ice cream is for when you have your tonsils out. Not for having your leg operated on."

He gave a satisfied nod, as if she'd said something profound. "That's so cool."

"What is?"

"That you know all that stuff. It's just...perfect."

"Why, thank you." She wondered where this was leading.

It didn't take long to find out, as Brady cocked his head to one side and said curiously, "So when are you and Daddy gonna get married?"

She stared at him, taken aback. Then she asked herself why she felt so surprised. She knew Brady was trying to promote a match between Alex and her. Obviously the child had seen the increased intimacy between them, even though he wasn't old enough to understand the dynamics behind it, and come to an understandable conclusion.

Which didn't make the correct response any clearer. Yet it didn't occur to her to try to dodge or palm him off with a platitude. After all, Brady wasn't only Alex's son; he was her buddy. "I don't know that we are, sweetie."

"What!" He jerked, making the air mattress jump. "Why not? You still like Daddy, don't you?"

"Of course I do."

"And I know he likes you. He's gotta. Otherwise, he wouldn't do all that mushy kissing stuff like you guys were doing yesterday on the ferry when you didn't think anybody was looking."

Shay felt the heat creep into her cheeks. She ignored it to gather her thoughts, then said carefully, "Just because two grown-ups like each other, that doesn't always mean they're going to get married, Brady."

He rolled his eyes impatiently. "I know *that*. But you guys aren't two grown-ups—you're *you* and Daddy's *Daddy*. And we need you." He said it as if that settled it.

She squeezed his hand. "Now, Brady—I think you're doing fine with your dad," she said firmly. "Look at all the good times you've had lately. He really cares about you. And I think—I hope—you know that no matter what happens with me and your dad, you and I will always be friends."

He shook his head. "I don't want to be friends," he said stubbornly. For once his young face, usually so filled with mischief, was deadly serious. "I want you to be my mom."

Shay felt as if a hand were squeezing her heart. "Oh, Brady—that's the nicest thing anybody ever said to me. And believe me, if I could marry just you and Nick and Mikey,

I'd do it in minute. But with adults, things are more complicated, sweetie.''

"Like how?"

"Well . . . you need to be compatible."

"What's that?"

"It means you get along. And you like lots of the same things."

"Well, you and Daddy like Nick and Mikey and me. And each other. That's what's important."

"Yes, but—" Shay frowned. He had an excellent point. She tried to think of a way to explain, wracking her brain for some of the things she hadn't liked about Alex at first.

Unfortunately, at the moment he seemed pretty perfect. "Well . . . we have different styles, different ways of doing things," she said finally, grasping at straws.

"Like what?"

"Well . . . your dad likes to get dressed up, and I prefer to be more casual. And he's pretty serious, while I'm . . . not. And he gets uptight sometimes, while I tend to be more laid back." She shrugged. "Besides, we haven't known each other very long. These things take time." It wasn't much of an answer, but it was the best she could do.

Thankfully, Mikey and Nick's sudden shrieks of excitement put an end to the conversation. Shay looked over and saw Alex had arrived at last and was standing in the cabana doorway.

He looked great, as usual. He'd loosened his tie and shucked the jacket of his elegant navy suit. As she watched, he took a step forward in his handmade Italian loafers, planted his feet and caught Mikey as the little boy flung himself forward. As Nick jumped up and down, clamoring for his turn, Alex swung the little boy high in the air, his broad shoulders straining against his crisp white shirt and dark suspenders. Ignoring the child's swimsuit, he then gave him a big hug.

Warmth stole through Shay, displacing the anxiety caused by Brady's questions. As uncertain as her and Alex's future might be, his relationship with the boys had undergone a decided change for the better the past few days. It was as if the passion they'd shared had burned away some sort of shell, freeing another Alex, one who was open and accessible to the people he cared about. No longer could he hold back the love and affection for the boys that he'd been keeping in reserve.

Shay watched, swamped with equal parts warmth, affection and tenderness as he set Mikey down, snatched up Nick and hugged him, too.

Both boys immediately demanded more. He chuckled and shook his head. "No way, guys. You're leaving wet footprints on my clothes." Grinning, he looked over, his gaze meeting Shay's across the width of the pool. "How are you?" he called.

"We're okay," Brady answered for her.

Alex raised an eyebrow. "That true?" he asked Shay.

He really did look great, his lean, elegant frame perfect for his beautifully tailored clothes. Desire joined the swirl of more virtuous emotions twining through her. "Yes."

The set of his shoulders tightened slightly at her husky tone. "Good. Are we still on for dinner?"

Shay tried to ignore a sudden flutter of nervousness. Thanks to Mrs. Rosencrantz, she and Alex were actually going out without the children that night. She knew it was ridiculous, but she felt like Cinderella must have when she'd faced her first formal function with the prince—excited, apprehensive, not quite certain what to expect.

"Shay? You aren't going to stand me up, are you?"

She pushed away her uncharacteristic insecurities and smiled. "No way."

"Thank God." He sent her a comical look of dismay as Nick reached up and grabbed a handful of white shirt in each hand.

"Swing me again, *please*, Daddy."

"Because—" he let out a loud growl, snatched the boy up and, much to Nick's giggling delight, hauled him over and dangled him over the pool "—between the office and these guys, I'm really looking forward to some civilized company!"

"Hey! That looks like fun!" Brady exclaimed. "Do me, Daddy!" Determined not to be left out, he rolled off the raft and struck out for the side.

The air mattress bucked wildly at the sudden shift of weight. Shay shrieked, tried to get a hand hold on the slippery vinyl...and failed. She heard Alex's laughter ring out—and then she tumbled into the water.

"Daddy?"

Alex paused in the middle of scraping the whiskers off his chin to glance at his eldest son. Brady was sitting on the bathroom counter, swinging his legs and generally keeping Alex company while he got ready for his date. "What?"

"Do you like Shay?"

Hadn't they had this conversation before? "Yes." He rinsed the razor, raised his chin and started on the underside of his jaw.

"She likes you, too."

He twisted his head to one side to get a better angle. "That's good."

"Except...do you have to be so serious? 'Cuz Shay would like you better if you weren't."

Alex's hand stilled. "How do you know that?"

"She told me."

He frowned. "Really?"

"Uh-huh. See, we were talking, before you got home, and when I asked her if you were gonna get married, she said—"

Alex's hand jerked. "Damn!" He yanked the razor away from his neck, grateful he hadn't cut his throat. His gaze shot to Brady. "You asked her if we were getting *married?*"

"Uh-huh."

He fixed the boy with his sternest look. "You were way out of line, young man."

"I was only trying to help," Brady protested. "I just thought—"

"Don't think," Alex admonished. "Every time you do, something goes wrong. If I decide to get married, *I'll* do the asking—okay?"

"But—" Brady started to argue, then subsided, his expression contrite as he took in the implacable look on his father's face. "'Kay. I'm sorry."

"It's all right. As long as you don't do it again." Alex resumed shaving. The room fell silent except for the steady scrape of the razor and the quiet thud of Brady's bare feet drumming against the cabinet.

Alex frowned at his reflection in the mirror. He'd done the right thing putting an end to the conversation. There were undoubtedly all sorts of ethical and moral reasons why it was wrong to pump an eight-year-old.

Of course, he hadn't really been pumping the boy. Brady had volunteered the information. And keeping the lines of communication open *was* a parental duty....

He sighed. "So what else did Shay say?"

Brady studied his toe. "About what?"

Alex's brow creased. "About... getting married."

"Well, she said she'd like to marry me and Mikey and Nick."

"Hmm. What about me?"

"Nope." The boy shook his head.

Nope? "Why not?"

"I dunno."

"She must've said something," Alex murmured.

"She said you were too serious."

"You already mentioned that."

"Well... I don't think she likes your clothes."

"She doesn't?"

"Uh-uh." Brady wagged his head glumly.

"Did she say what she didn't like?""

The boy picked up Alex's after-shave, smelled it and made a face. "Too dressy."

"Oh." Alex looked lovingly at his Armani suit hanging on the door and wondered how anyone could find it offensive. "Anything else?"

"Nope. Oh... except for that stuff about how she's laid back, but you're kind of... uptight."

He stared at Brady in surprise. "She said that?"

"Uh-huh."

"That's ridiculous. I'm not uptight. Do you think I'm uptight?"

"Uh-uh. If I was a girl, *I'd* marry you, Daddy," he added loyally.

"Yeah, me too," Alex muttered. His expression preoccupied, he stroked the razor across his face one last time, set it down, dropped his towel and headed for the shower. "I may be a lot of things, but I am *not* uptight."

Brady waited until the glass door swung shut and the steam started to crest over the top of the shower before he turned back to the mirror. He looked around, then turned on the tap, splashed warm water on his face, picked up Alex's shaving cream and sprayed a puff the size of a grapefruit into the palm of his hand. He slapped it on his face, popped the blade out of Alex's razor and began to shave.

From the shower, Alex could be heard talking to himself. "Conservative? Maybe. But uptight? I don't think so...."

With an air of supreme satisfaction, Brady stopped shaving. He winked at his reflection. Shay was right. No matter what Daddy said, he was too uptight.

It was just lucky for him he had a wonderful son who'd found the perfect wife to help him get over it.

"Alex?"

Shay stood in the cottage doorway and tried not to gape at her dinner date. For the first time since she'd met him, Alex Morrison was wearing jeans. Not only that, but he was also wearing loafers without socks, an open-throated denim shirt under a casual white sport coat, and gold-rimmed aviator sunglasses.

The look suited him to a T, although Shay had a feeling it was his own innate elegance that gave the outfit its chic, sexy distinction, and not the other way around.

Whatever the reason, he looked stunning.

He also looked more than a little stunned. "Shay?" Despite the dark lenses shielding his eyes, his tone revealed his surprise. "You look... fabulous."

She sent him an impish grin, fingering the clinging sleeve of the brief, black stretch-lace dress she'd paired with sheer black nylons and high, high heels. Diamonds glinted in her ears and at the end of a gold neck chain, her hair was swept back and *she* was wearing makeup for a change. "You don't have to sound so surprised."

He looked immediately contrite. "Aw, hell—I'm sorry. I didn't mean—" He ran a hand through his hair, giving it a slightly windblown look that was perfect with his outfit. "I didn't mean it the way it came out. It's just... I had this crazy idea you might enjoy doing something more...casual tonight. Something that wasn't so serious. I thought we'd have dinner on the pier in town. Afterward, we could take in the boardwalk and the arcade. I've never been, but I understand it's first-rate." His gaze flickered over her, lingering for a flattering amount of time on the length of her legs. "Then again, it will just take me a minute to change and—"

"It sounds great," she cut in. She stepped back and gestured him to enter. "Lucky for you, I'm not quite ready. Come on in and make yourself comfortable while I finish."

Before he had a chance to utter the protest she could see forming on his lips, she crossed the room and sailed into the bathroom. She allowed herself a moment to smile at the irony of the situation—*she* was too overdressed for Alex?— then turned to the mirror, debating her course of action.

She looked critically at her reflection. Alex was right—she did look nice even though she was clearly dressed too formally for what he had in mind. Still, she had paid a fortune for this dress—and it was the only really nice thing she owned. Maybe, with just a few slight changes...

She rejoined Alex less than five minutes later. She'd exchanged the diamond necklace for a black ribbon choker, her dark hosiery for bare legs, her high heels for little black flats and brushed her dark hair into a casual, almost boyish look that tumbled over her brow.

To her delight, his expression filled with a combination of admiration and appreciation when he saw her. "I'm not sure what you did, but you look great."

"Thanks. So do you."

He blinked at the compliment, then a crooked smile crept across his face.

"Ready?" she said breezily. She picked up her purse, a tiny black brocade bag on a long silk cord.

"You're something else," he murmured, as she locked the cottage and they walked out to the Mercedes.

The next few hours were some of the most enjoyable of Shay's life. They had dinner at a small open-air café on the pier. Over steaming baskets of fish and chips, Alex told her about his day. Somehow, that led to a discussion of his childhood and how he'd grown up riding herd over Beau and James at the Olympiana Resort his parents had managed on Washington's southwest coast. He'd told her how he'd taken the small inheritance he'd received when his dad passed away and made a killing in the futures market, earning enough to buy his first resort. And, after she made it clear she really wanted to know, he shared the adventures of his sons' births, displaying a wicked sense of humor as he poked fun at his own squeamishness.

They were still talking long after sunset, which was when Shay finally shared her own big news. "I've had an offer to do a book," she said during a lull in the conversation.

Alex went very still. "What?"

She made no effort to hide the anticipation, excitement and apprehension she felt. "They want to reprint the stories I did on various world hot spots—Bosnia, Rwanda, Haiti, Russia—and have me do an accompanying commentary on what was going on behind the scenes at the time—the rumors, the mood, what followed. Sort of the story behind the story. I've said . . . yes."

For a long moment he simply stared at her. And then his face lit up with a smile that made her toes curl in her shoes. "That's terrific."

"I know."

"Come on, I'll buy you an ice-cream cone to celebrate."

They did just that, purchasing double scoops of ice cream from a shop along the boardwalk. "So, what do you think?" Alex said as they strolled along amidst a smattering of other tourists, engaged as they were in checking out the colorful window displays and enjoying the warm summer evening. "Are you having a nice time?"

"Absolutely," she said truthfully. They stopped to examine a display of Native American pottery. "Although, I have to admit I'm curious. Are you ever going to tell me what inspired this?"

He glanced blandly down at her upturned face. "What do you mean?"

"Oh, I don't know. It just seems to me that dinner at Harbor House—" the area's most exclusive restaurant "—in an Armani suit is more your style."

He pursed his lips. For a moment she was afraid she'd offended him, but then the corners of his golden eyes turned up. "You know me pretty well, don't you?" he murmured. He reached out to take her hand.

An undeniable thrill went through her. She sent him a mischievous grin as they once more began to meander along, her fingers linked securely with his. "Either that, or I'm psychic."

The smile spread from his eyes to his lips. "I don't think so. If you were, you wouldn't always ask so many questions."

She stopped walking. "Are you saying I'm nosy?"

"No." He tugged on her hand to get her moving again, then put his arm around her, resting his palm on the small of her back. "*Impudent* is the word that comes to mind."

"Are you going to tell me or not?"

He grinned. "It was Brady."

"Gosh. Why aren't I surprised?"

"He seemed to think you'd like me better if I loosened up. So I ironed my old jeans—"

She made a sound midway between a chuckle and a groan. "Oh, Alex. You *ironed* your jeans?"

He shrugged. "What else could I do? Mrs. Rosencrantz refused. Now, as I was saying, I ironed my jeans, canceled our reservation—at Harbor House—and here we are."

"We were going to have dinner at Harbor House? Oh, no!"

"Hey, it serves you right for telling Brady I was tense, somber and a stuffy dresser."

"That isn't what I said," she protested.

He raised one dark eyebrow. "Really?"

"Well . . . not exactly."

His eyes glinted. "I have to admit I am curious," he said wryly, echoing her earlier statement. "Are you going to tell me what inspired such slander—or not?"

She adopted a put-upon air. "I was trying to save your bacon, Morrison. Your eldest son is plotting to give you away in marriage, and I was merely trying to point out to him why I'm not a suitable candidate. I made a few comparisons, that's all. It's not my fault he's more concerned with *your* deficiencies than mine."

"That might be true—if I had any deficiencies."

She gave a hoot. "Oh, dear. Perfect . . . and modest, too. That kind of ego deserves a prize. Come on, I'll win you a teddy bear." She indicated a booth where a fast-talking young man was using a cork-shooting air rifle to demonstrate how "easy" it was to knock over the ducks and geese on the moving display.

Alex made a face. "For a reporter, you're awfully naive. It's fixed."

She made a tsking sound. "Of course it is. It wouldn't be a challenge, otherwise. It's just a matter of figuring out how it's rigged and then beating them at their own game. Watch."

She fluffed her hair, wet her lips, hitched up her dress, and sauntered toward the booth, staring in wide-eyed admiration at the carny. "Gee. You must be really smart," she simpered, rummaging around in her tiny purse. She pulled out several ten-dollar bills, her manner suggesting she had an IQ only slightly higher than a rutabaga's. "Do you think you could show me how to do that?"

The young man looked like a hungry cat who'd spotted an unprotected canary. "I'd be happy to show *you* all my tricks," he purred, with a greedy glance at her lithe little body.

Alex stood where he was and watched. On the one hand, he felt amused by Shay's audacity. On the other, he felt a compelling urge to knock the other man's teeth down his throat for coming on to her.

His mixed feelings increased when she leaned over to shoot the rifle and her dress rose alarmingly. He swallowed, a burst of heat going through him as he studied her fanny in the clinging lace and realized just how smoothly it flowed over her compact curves. It couldn't hug her more closely if she'd forgotten to put on her underwear....

Good God. The burst of heat became a fiery blaze that seared him like an out-of-control flamethrower, branding him with a host of distinctly primitive emotions. Without knowing how he got there, he suddenly found himself at Shay's side just as the carny, looking more than a little bewildered, reached forward to hand her the large pink teddy bear she'd effortlessly won.

"Excuse me." Alex snatched the stuffed animal from the other man's nerveless fingers. "But I believe this is mine."

The look he turned on Shay as he grabbed her hand and hauled her away made it clear he wasn't talking bears.

"Alex! What are you doing?" she demanded, laughing. "I was just getting warmed up. Another ten minutes and I would've had a bear for each of the boys."

"Forget bears," he said tersely. He set off for the Mercedes at a killer pace.

"Well, for heaven's sake!" She dug in her heels. "Where's the fire?"

He stopped and did something he'd never done before in his life. Heedless of the hoots and stares of a host of amused onlookers, he tossed the pink teddy bear to the ground and swept her into his arms. "Guess," he rasped. And then, right there in plain sight of God and Port Sandy, he kissed her. Heatedly. Carnally. Thoroughly. By the time he finally raised his head, she was trembling like a chandelier in an earthquake.

Shay stared up into Alex's passion-glazed eyes, which glittered in the dark like twin gold flames. "Well," she said weakly. "I guess that answers my question. Maybe we'd better go home before we burn down the town."

She didn't have to make the suggestion twice.

Eleven

"**Y**ou make me crazy," Alex murmured against Shay's throat.

They were the first words he'd spoken since that incredible kiss on the boardwalk. They stood locked together, just inside the cottage doorway, which was as far as they'd made it after a tense drive home that had probably set a new land-speed record.

"The feeling's mutual," she said with a gasp as, without warning, he stroked his hands down her thighs all the way to her knees—then ran them back up under the hem of her dress.

"Damn!" He closed his big warm hands around the cool bare flesh of her derriere and exhaled explosively. "I *knew* it!"

"Knew what?"

"That you were out to get to me," he rasped. Hungry for her taste, he raked his teeth against the underside of her jaw, then licked away the slight sting with a strong stroke of his tongue. "Haven't you ever heard of underwear?"

"Of course," she said indignantly. Or as indignantly as she could, given the erotic way he was massaging her with his fingertips. "It's your fault I'm not wearing any."

He groaned. "*My* fault? God. Don't I wish—"

"It is," she insisted. "I was wearing panty hose when you got here, remember? And then when I went to change... Well, I guess I forgot in the rush to get going."

"You forgot? Lord help me."

"Is that what this is all about?"

"Don't forget anymore, okay? I don't think my heart can take the strain. Not to mention a certain other part of me."

"That certain other part doesn't feel as if it's suffering to me. In fact—" she slowly rotated her hips, wondering as she did where this daring, outrageous, blatantly physical side of her had been hiding all these years "—it feels terrific. Except—" She let the single word dangle.

"Except *what?*"

"You're overdressed. As usual."

"Lady, tonight is your lucky night. I can definitely take care of that." Suiting action to words, he let go of her long enough to toe off his shoes, unfasten his jeans, slide them and his boxers down and kick them away. Clad in nothing but his soft denim shirt, he leaned down and kissed her fervently on the mouth.

Shay welcomed him eagerly. She parted her lips, nipped his bottom lip, then slanted her head to deepen the kiss. And all the while her hands skated over him, tickling his ribs, skimming his flanks and belly, until finally she grew bold enough to measure the hot male length of him with her palms. "Oh, yes.... That's certainly... better," she murmured.

He inhaled noisily. Grasping her wrists, he drew her hands up and pressed them against his chest. "You're a menace. Any more of that and things will be over before they start."

He was trembling. The discovery unleashed a flood of tenderness that made her desperate to touch him. Tugging her hands free of his grip, she reached around and ran them up under his shirt. His skin was hot, the lean muscles in his back, tense. She explored each warm curve, each firm hollow, urging him closer as she followed the path of his spine from his nape to his tailbone.

He shuddered. "Shay..." He cupped her lace-covered breasts and pressed them together, lashing the aching tips of her nipples with his thumbs. "So sweet..."

She arched her back, moaning with her need for him. "Now, Alex. *Now.*"

He didn't need further encouragement. With a harsh, primitive sound, he yanked her dress up and wrapped his arms around her. "Lock your hands around my neck and hold on," he started to tell her, only to find she'd already anticipated his request.

He lifted her up and, with one powerful thrust, filled her.

They both cried out at the first jabbing glide of connection.

"You feel so good," he murmured, his voice ragged with pleasure as she locked her legs around his waist. Slowly his shoulders lifted and his buttocks flexed.

He began a forceful rhythm that stole what little breath she had left. "Oh, Alex, *yes*—just like that." She threaded her fingers through his hair and arched back, bracing her shoulders against the door. "Don't stop. *Don't. Stop.*"

"As if I could..."

She wanted, she *needed* to see him. She forced her eyes open and found herself held spellbound by the stark beauty of his very masculine face. His lashes were thick and spiky against the sharply chiseled planes of his cheeks. His nose was a strong, straight blade above the sensual curve of his mouth. His teeth were clenched, gritted with effort as he relentlessly increased the pace of each long thrust and withdrawal.

The sight of him, his skin golden in the dim light, his teeth white, his sun-streaked hair tumbled over his brow, triggered a pleasure in Shay so deep it almost hurt. It moved through her in a slow flood, gathering strength like a river rushing downstream. She gave herself up to it, letting it carry her from torrent to flood tide.

And all the time, she never took her eyes from Alex. Through a satisfaction so sweet it made her eyes sting, she watched him. She watched the skin tighten across his cheeks. She watched the perspiration dampen his hair and sheen his skin. She watched a savage concentration steal over his elegant features, as his lips parted, his face contorted and his entire body quaked with his final thrust.

The sight was so profound, his pleasure became her own, until she didn't know where he ended and she began. Love and heat, desire and need, all washed through her. She let it sweep her away and tumble her through a dark sweet current.

When she came back to herself, Alex was sitting on the floor with his back to the door, and she was cradled sideways across his lap. The solid beat of his heart pounded under her ear, the sound steadily slowing as his breathing evened out.

"You okay?" he asked hoarsely, gently stroking a hand through her hair.

It felt heavenly. So did being cuddled against him. She gave a satisfied sigh. "I'm fine."

"Sure?"

She pressed a kiss to his collarbone. His shirt hung open. Curious—she didn't remember either one of them unbuttoning it—she ran her fingers down the placket.

All the buttons but one were gone, and it was hanging by a thread. Her mouth tipped up.

"You want to go to the zoo tomorrow?" he asked out of the blue.

Shay tipped her head up in surprise. "Is that an invitation? Or an editorial comment?"

His mouth quirked. "Invitation. I forgot to ask earlier. I have to go into the office to sign some papers. It'll just take a minute, so I thought as long as I was making the trip, we could take the boys." He paused, then added thoughtfully, "Although, now that you've pointed it out, I guess you do have certain animalistic qualities."

She leaned back and narrowed her eyes at him. "Like *what?*"

He widened his eyes in mock alarm. "Hey... simmer down." He grinned when she socked him, then assumed a wounded pose. "All I was going to say was that you're what we called a fox when I was in high school."

For a long moment she didn't say a word. And then she began to chuckle. "*Fox?* Oh, Alex, that's so sweet, but—where have you been? Nobody says *fox* anymore. You either say someone is hot or fine or bad—or in a pinch, I suppose you could call them a babe."

He snorted. "Okay. I can do that. Hey, *you hot, fine, bad babe*—you want to go to the damn zoo or not?"

"Oh, d-dear," she sputtered. "How can I resist when you p-put it like that?" The chuckle turned into a full-bodied laugh.

Alex sighed. It was clear he had no choice. He was simply going to have to sacrifice himself and make love to her again to shut her up.

Only this time he was damn well going to make sure they made it to the bed before things got out of hand.

"I wish you could stay all night," Shay said, yawning sleepily as she snuggled closer to Alex. He was lying flat on his back, with her stretched out on top of him—the best they could manage on the narrow sofa, which was as far as they'd gotten before they'd made love a second time.

With a satiated sigh she settled her cheek more comfortably into the crook of his neck and threaded her fingers through the dark gold curls on his chest.

"Me, too," Alex said quietly. "Me, too."

The amazing thing was, he meant it.

He was tired of sleeping alone. He was tired of waking up without her in his arms, of always making love in the dark, of not having the right to haul her into his bedroom in broad daylight and lock the door.

And that wasn't all. He was tired of *being* alone. Hell—who was he kidding? As great as the sex was—and it was pretty damn great, unlike anything he'd ever experienced—it was just a small part of what he missed each time he had to go back to his house without her.

He missed her laughter. He missed having her to talk to, whether it was about the boys or the world or the state of the weather. He missed seeing her with the kids and the way her big dark eyes gleamed when something amused her. He even missed having her around to take him down a notch on the rare occasions he needed it.

He sighed, tightening his arms around her to make sure she didn't roll off onto the floor as she drifted off to sleep.

There was no getting around it. She was not just the best lover he'd ever had. She was also quickly becoming his best friend.

So what the hell are you waiting for? Why don't you put an end to your misery and marry her?

He blinked—and then dismissed the idea as being too ridiculous to warrant a second thought. Laughter, friendship and killer sex were hardly the basis for marriage.

Oh yeah? Why not? There are plenty of people who do just fine with less.

He frowned. Even though that might be true, the last thing he wanted was a wife; he'd decided that after Ali died. This entire train of thought was simply the result of his subconscious working overtime after that discussion with Brady about marriage.

Except…getting married again would certainly solve the problem of sleeping alone.

Not to mention taking care of the nanny problem once and for all.

And it would certainly make the boys happy.

And what better candidate than Shay? He knew he hadn't known her very long, but then again, he'd known that Allison was right for him the first time he'd seen her.

Of course, he wasn't in love with Shay, he was quick to tell himself, staving off the twist of anxiety that curled through him at the thought. Not that he didn't feel *something* for her. He did. He felt affection, admiration, respect, even a certain devotion. And he trusted her, to a depth that would have surprised him four weeks ago. But then, that was before he'd spent such concentrated time with the boys and discovered that it was the civilian equivalent to military combat. The way he figured it, he and Shay had gone through the sort of heightened contact and intense mutual reliance that bonded comrades together for life.

Still... The sudden change in his thinking puzzled him. He searched his mind for the cause, until it dawned on him her announcement about her new job had made the difference. Up until then there'd been a part of him, acknowledged or not, that had always expected her to return to frontline reporting, a career choice that simply didn't lend itself to being part of a home and family.

But now that was no longer a barrier. Now, he could finally admit how much he wanted, even needed her, in his life.

Marriage was the perfect solution. He got an interesting, independent, sexy companion who would never bore him. The boys got a mom. And Shay got the roots, the permanence, the family life she'd missed out on while she was growing up.

He lay there for a while, savoring the anticipation spiraling through him now that he'd made the decision. He'd make her a good husband, he vowed. He might not love her, exactly, but he cared. A lot. Maybe they'd even have a baby. A little girl with big brown eyes and her mother's mischievous smile....

He'd ask her tomorrow, he decided, after they got back from the zoo. Maybe they'd wait a few days before they told the boys. He smiled. It would make the perfect gift for Brady's birthday. He could just imagine his son's reaction. The kid would probably take full credit for bringing them together and be impossible to live with for months.

Suddenly eager to get home and get to sleep so that morning would come, he gathered Shay against him, sat up and carefully stood.

"Umm..." Her voice fuzzy with sleep, Shay opened her eyes and regarded him drowsily. "Alex?"

"Shh," he whispered, carrying her to the bed. "Go back to sleep. Everything's fine."

Everything was perfect.

Shay gave a sigh of pleasure and leaned back against the Mercedes's butter-soft leather seat. She smiled at the chorus of snores issuing from the back seat, where the boys were fast asleep. The last time she'd looked they'd been tumbled together like three exhausted puppies, leaning one against the other as close as their seat belts would allow.

It had been a long day. They must have walked a hundred miles along Woodland Park Zoo's meandering trails. And she'd enjoyed every inch.

True, her feet hurt, her nose was sunburned and there was a prominent mustard stain on her T-shirt. But that was a small price to pay for the fun she'd had. She'd laughed with Brady, Nick, Mikey and Alex at the monkeys' antics, oohed and aahed over the lions and tigers in the African savannah and stood for more than half an hour watching the hippos swim in their pool, expressing suitable amazement at how graceful the stumpy creatures were in the water.

The kids had been cheerful, cooperative and kind to each other. There'd been a few tense moments when she and Alex had misplaced Mikey in the Nocturnal House, but they'd quickly found him staring wide-eyed at an opossum, and the crisis had been averted. Alex had even brought his camera and, much to Shay's unspoken delight, taken her picture along with the boys as if she were a member of the family.

She slanted a glance sideways, her contentment taking on a wry twist as she looked at him.

He took his eyes off the road long enough to meet her gaze. One dark eyebrow rose. "What?"

Her mouth quirked. "Nothing, really. I was just thinking you're the only person I know who could—and would—wear white slacks and an ice blue polo shirt for this kind of excursion, and wind up looking as good when it was over as when he started."

He looked surprised, and then his face relaxed into a wry smile. "It used to drive Beau nuts when we were kids. No matter what we did, at the end of the day he looked like he'd just climbed out of a mud hole while *I* looked the same way I had when I went out the door." His smile took on a definite tinge of satisfaction that Shay imagined had something to do with the mysterious world of siblings. "It still bugs him. He claims it's one of life's great mysteries. Like the Bermuda Triangle or how come your fingers and toes wrinkle in the bathtub when the rest of you doesn't."

"I don't know about the Bermuda Triangle, but the reason your fingers shrivel is because the tips are covered with a thicker layer of skin than the rest of you," she said idly. "When you soak, it absorbs water and expands, only there's no place for it to go. So it buckles—like an asphalt road in the summer heat."

He turned to stare at her in surprise. "You're kidding. It's that simple?" When she nodded, he shook his head. "You know the darnedest stuff."

Shay smiled, feeling ridiculously pleased. She'd never loved him more than she did at that moment, when he was so relaxed and open. It was as if something had changed in the past twenty-four hours. She couldn't quite put her finger on it, but the way he was acting reminded her of something.

No, that wasn't right. It wasn't something, she realized, it was someone. *Brady,* to be precise. Alex had the same sort of barely contained exuberance that his oldest son got when he was hatching a plot or harboring some wonderful secret that he was waiting for just the right moment to spring on someone.

Intrigued, she examined him a little more closely, noting the good humor alive in the curve of his sculpted lips and the energetic way his finger tapped the steering wheel. Something was definitely going on.

Shay shook her head and decided she wasn't going to let herself get *too* curious. If she let herself dwell on it, it would make her crazy. Besides, most likely it had something to do with Brady's birthday, which was only a few days away.

"Speaking of Beau, he called this morning," Alex said.

She sat up in surprise. "He did?"

"Yes." He glanced in the rearview mirror, double checking to make sure all three boys were still asleep. He lowered his voice. "He's flying in for Brady's birthday," he whispered, barely audible over the air conditioner. "We had a terrible connection, but he claims he's bringing him a special present, something he says Brady really wants. He said to say hi."

There was a gleam in his eye that suggested Beau had said more than that, but judging from his expression he wasn't about to say what, so again she let it go.

Besides, she had a more pressing problem. "Good grief. I suppose he's going to need the cottage back." She bit her lip, staring out at the trees that lined one side of the road as they took the Port Sandy exit. She was surprised at the distress that shot through her.

Alex reached over and patted her bare knee. "Don't worry about it. Either he can stay at the house or—" he only hesitated for a second "—you can."

Her distress dissolved, replaced by surprise. "But—"

"Are we almost home?" Brady's sleepy voice interrupted. "I'm thirsty."

Shay twisted around, her expression softening when she got a clear view of his tonsils as he gave an enormous yawn.

Beside him, Nick stirred as well, his thick, dark blond lashes fluttering up. "Me, too. And I'm hungry. Real hungry. Can we stop somewhere?"

Alex shook his head. "How can you be hungry? You had a double stack of pancakes for breakfast. And two hot dogs, a snow cone, some cotton candy, a bag of popcorn, and two soda pops at the zoo."

"I dunno. I just am."

While Alex contemplated that, Mikey decided the issue. "Daddy?"

"What?"

"I only had one cola," the four-year-old said shyly. "But I've really got to... you know."

Alex knew when he was beat. "I guess we could stop at the Mini-mart."

"Oh, boy!" Nick and Brady both chortled as they saw the sign up ahead. "Can we get slushies? Please, Daddy?"

Alex rolled his eyes as he turned and drove up the short, sloping parking lot. He stopped in front of the store and set the emergency brake against the incline.

All three boys were out of the car and into the store before he'd unsnapped his seat belt. He turned and looked at Shay. "You coming?"

She leaned her head back against the head rest and closed her eyes. "I think I'll pass."

"Coward."

She smiled, listening as he climbed out and shut the door. She waited a heartbeat, then opened her eyes to admire the view as he walked away, watching him as he went inside and herded the kids out of sight toward the rest rooms.

She yawned and looked around.

The only other car in the lot was an old station wagon parked to her right. She frowned. Not only were the windows down, but some idiot had left a toddler unattended in the front seat.

True, the little boy, who looked to be a year or two younger than Mikey, was secured in a car seat, but still... Anyone could come along and take the tyke. Or the child could get loose and burn himself on the cigarette lighter or something. Shay glanced at the store, tempted to go inside, find whoever was responsible and tell them in no uncertain terms the risk they were taking.

She looked back at the child, who had a halo of taffy-colored curls and big dark eyes. He grinned a good-natured baby grin and waved. She waggled her fingers and again turned her attention to the store, pursing her lips in disapproval as she caught sight of a gum-chewing teenage girl flirting with the young store clerk.

A minute passed. Maybe two. Shay was still glowering at the unsuspecting girl when Alex and the boys appeared, headed for the slushie machine.

Just the sight of them—her own little group—soothed her. Maybe she wouldn't completely blast Miss Gum when the girl finally came out. Maybe she'd let her off with the condensed version of the riot act. After all, no real harm had been done—

She caught a flash of motion out of the corner of her eye. Swiveling around, she was just in time to see the station wagon start to roll backward down the slope. Free of his car seat, the toddler stood at the wheel, looking surprised.

Shay didn't stop to think. She threw open the door and took off after him.

Twelve

"Okay, Michael. Push the button. Now."

His lower lip caught between his teeth in concentration, Mikey leaned over from his position straddling Alex's hip and hit the switch on the slushie machine.

A neon green stream gushed into the cup Alex was holding under the spout. He didn't want to think about what went into the mixture to make it that color; sometimes ignorance truly was bliss. "Okay. That's good."

Mikey looked up. "What did you say, Daddy?"

Alex grimaced as the icy green stream spilled over the cup top and covered his hand. "*Stop.*"

"Okay." Mikey released the button and straightened.

Alex lowered the boy to the ground, grabbed some paper napkins, wiped off the cup and handed it to him.

The boy beamed. "Did I do good?"

Alex smiled back. "You did great." He flexed his fingers, sighed at the sticky residue that remained and glanced over at Brady and Nick, who were perusing comic books while they noisily slurped slushies the color of a nuclear sunset. "Watch your brother," he told the pair. "Do *not* move from that spot. I'm going to go wash my hands."

"Sure," they said amiably.

When he came back, they were nowhere in sight.

Not only that, but neither was the clerk or the other customer.

Alex's internal alarm clamored as if faced with a five-alarm fire. After one more swift look around to make sure the little miscreants weren't hiding somewhere, he loped toward the door, his mind racing as he wondered what the heck they'd done now. Robbed the place? Taken everyone hostage? Tried to hijack the slushie machine?

It didn't matter, he decided grimly, stiff-arming the door. Even if they'd just gone out to get in the car, they were in big trouble.

After all, it wasn't as if he'd asked that much. How much effort did it take to stay put for three minutes? Particularly when *he'd* been making a real attempt to be a better dad. Wasn't he letting them drink scary stuff made of food dyes and chemical additives? Hadn't he'd taken them to the zoo? Wasn't he even willing to get married to get them the mom they wanted, which would be a whole hell of a lot easier if only—

If only the potential mom in question wasn't hanging half-in and half-out of a strange car that happened to be hurtling down the hill toward the main road.

Alex paled. *"What the hell?"*

"Isn't it cool, Daddy!" Brady cried. He and the other boys raced over from where they'd been standing on the walkway, next to the spot where the store clerk was trying to console a hysterical young woman who was chewing a huge wad of gum and crying.

"It's just like 'Rescue 911'! Shay's gonna save that girl's baby brother!"

Yeah, right—as long as she doesn't get herself killed first, Alex thought, nearly having heart failure as the car hit a bump and Shay was thrown into the air, barely managing to hang on. *"Stay here!"* he shouted to the boys, in a tone that promised dire consequences if they even *thought* about ignoring him. With that, he tore down the hill, nominally aware of the store clerk and the girl hot on his heels.

As seemed to be the case in most of Alex's dealings with Shay, she was one step ahead of him. All he could do was chase after her, close enough to see what was happening but too far away to do anything.

While he looked on helplessly, she squirmed, trying to wedge her way deeper into the car. Suddenly she hitched up her knees and pitched forward far enough to push the squalling toddler down on the seat and get a hand on the steering wheel. She gave it a wrench; the car slued sideways. From Alex's vantage point it seemed to slide forever before the tires finally caught and the vehicle swung right, shooting onto the shoulder of the road with Shay clinging for dear life.

The station wagon rolled backward for a dozen yards before it stopped, safely out of the way of oncoming traffic. Alex skidded to a stop in a spray of gravel next to the driver's door. Panting, he bent his head, braced his hands on his knees and caught his breath, then reached over and hauled Shay out of the window opening. He pulled her clear as the store clerk and the still-weeping girl arrived. Sobbing with relief, the latter snatched open the car door and scooped up the toddler, hugging the little boy fiercely.

Alex cupped Shay's shoulders in his hands and gave her a quick once-over. "Are you all right?" he asked urgently.

She stared blankly at him. "Alex?"

"Are you hurt?"

She sent him a faint smile. "No. No, of course not." She held up both hands, gallantly ignoring the fact they were shaking as if palsied. "See? Not a scratch."

At that moment, the teenage girl whose negligence had almost resulted in tragedy walked over, the toddler clutched in her arms. "Thank you," she said fervently, reaching out and awkwardly squeezing Shay's hand. "If something had happened to Curtis, I don't know what I would have done...."

Her voice broke and the store clerk said soothingly, "Come on, Carrie. We'd better go call your folks. I don't think you'd better drive."

"I guess you're right," Carrie replied, her shoulders drooping. With a final squeeze of Shay's hand, she turned and followed the young man back up the hill.

Clearly impatient with the interruption, Alex said quickly to Shay, "Are you *sure* you're okay?"

"I'm fine."

"Thank God." He lifted her off her feet and crushed her against him in a hug so fervent it was a miracle he didn't crack her ribs. "Dammit, you took ten years off my life!" He buried his face in her hair. "Don't you know that I—" He took a deep breath and swallowed hard. "That I..."

"What?" she said breathlessly.

An enormous shudder racked him. "That I think that was absolutely, positively, beyond question, the most stupid, irresponsible, lame-brained stunt I ever saw!" he said furiously, setting her away from him so fast she was lucky not to get whiplash.

She blinked. For a moment there, she would have sworn he'd been about to tell her he loved her. *"What?"*

"You're lucky you weren't killed! Who the *hell* do you think you are? Arnold Schwartzeneggerette?"

Her mouth dropped. "Excuse me?"

"You heard me!" he roared.

"Everyone in the county can hear you!"

"Don't change the subject! Answer the question! What the devil did you think you were doing?"

She took a deep breath. "I was doing exactly what I set out to do—stop a runaway car from rolling into the street with a child in it."

"Oh, yeah?" He said it as if she'd confessed to running naked through the streets of Port Sandy.

"Yeah."

"Well, what if something had gone wrong? What if that car had been equipped with a locking steering wheel and it had shot onto the road with you in it? And been hit by a logging truck or something!"

"But it didn't!"

"Or what if you'd lost your grip and fallen? Did you think about that!"

"But that's not what happened!"

"Well, it could have—which *you* obviously never stopped to consider! You could've been killed! But did you care? Hell, no. You just went racing off, without a thought to the consequences—"

Shay couldn't believe it. "Oh, for heaven's sake! What should I have done? Stood by and watched while that little kid got creamed?" She shook her head in disbelief. "That's the most ridiculous thing I've ever heard."

Alex's eyes turned as hard as golden bullets. "Well, pardon me! Am I boring you with my silly fears? But then, I forgot—this kind of escapade is second nature to you, isn't it? I thought, when you said you were going to do the book, that there might actually be a future for us, but now—"

"*What?*" she squeaked.

"*Now* I can see I was wrong! I suppose I ought to be grateful that I found out *now,* instead of after I proposed! Because obviously, leopards don't change their stripes!"

"It's spots," she said automatically, trying to decide whether or not he'd really just said what she thought he had.

He sent her an incredulous look. "That's it! It's over. I'm done." He turned on his heel and stormed up the hill.

Stunned, she stood looking after him, trying to understand what had just happened. It was clear he'd had a scare—but then, so had she. Still, unless she was hallucinating, he'd just withdrawn a marriage proposal he'd never made in the first place!

She took a deep breath, shook her head to clear it and took off after him. Before she could catch him, however, the boys came racing toward her, demanding her attention as they all spoke at once.

"That was so cool!"

"Yeah! It was just like in the movies!"

"You oughta be on TV."

Hanging on her arms and legs as she led the way toward the car, they touched and patted her, making sure she was okay at the same time they voiced their pride in her.

"That was really, really brave."

"Were you ascared?"

"I bet that car was going a hundred miles an hour!"

"Naw—I bet it was going two hundred!"

"You're a real hero!"

"That's enough, boys," Alex said curtly, opening the back door as they reached the Mercedes. "Get in the car and fasten your seat belts."

All four of them turned to look at him.

"Well? What are you staring at? Get in the car!"

"But, Dad—"

"Now!"

The boys' eyes went wide. For a moment they didn't move. But then they took a good look at his expression. They piled into the Mercedes with alacrity.

Without so much as a glance at Shay, Alex slammed the door, opened his, climbed in and started the engine.

She hurried around the car. She didn't think he'd drive off without her, but she wasn't willing to put it to a test. The loony way he was acting, anything was possible.

"I don't see why you're so mad," Brady was saying as she got in—a sentiment after her own heart.

Alex's voice was icy. "Drop it."

"I mean, it was so cool. I saw this guy on "Rescue 911" do the same thing—only *he* got run over."

Alex shot Shay a speaking glance. "That doesn't surprise me a bit."

"Now, wait one—" she began.

"Gee, Daddy—" Brady said at the same time.

"I don't want to hear another word. From *anybody*," Alex snapped.

Shay folded her arms across her chest. Although it took an effort, she managed to keep her mouth shut. Despite what Alex thought, she did value her life, enough not to challenge him in his current mood. Besides—there were now several things she wanted to say to him that were definitely not suitable for their current audience.

The drive home was made in tense silence. Alex pulled around to the back of the house, stopped the car, and everyone climbed out.

"Go find Mrs. Rosencrantz," Shay told the boys.

"'Kay." Mikey and Nick raced off toward the kitchen.

Brady didn't move. "But—"

"Please?"

He looked from her to his Dad and back again. His shoulders slumped. "'Kay," he said reluctantly. Feet dragging, he started off.

Alex sent her a tight-lipped glance. "Thank you, Ms. Spenser, for minding *my* business. As usual." He stalked away toward the patio, stomped across it, unlocked the cabana and disappeared inside.

Shay rolled her eyes and marched after him.

By the time she reached the pool, he was standing at the side with the long-handled net, skimming leaves and other debris from the water's bright blue surface.

She put her hands on her hips. "You know, as cute as your fanny is, I'm getting awfully tired of chasing after it."

He didn't look up. "Trust me, the feeling is mutual." He swept up a dead grasshopper and dumped it on the concrete at her feet.

She glared at him. "So are you going to tell me what's going on? Why you're so angry? And what you meant by those things you said about...us?"

"No."

"Alex," she said warningly.

He looked up, his expression guarded. "Just forget it, okay? I was out of line, talking to you the way I did. I apologize. That's it."

"No, it's not."

"Oh, really?" He shrugged with exaggerated patience. "Have it your way. You want it spelled out? I was going to ask you to marry me. Now I'm not."

He sounded remarkably like one of his sons at that moment, Shay decided. That was exactly the tone they used when things weren't going their way and they announced the game was over, they were packing up their marbles and going home. She had no intention of letting Alex off so easy, however. "Why not?" she said flatly.

"Why not? Because I owe it to the boys to choose a wife who's going to be around for a while, that's why! Someone who doesn't go chasing after danger. Someone who isn't going to get herself killed right under their noses! They've already lost one mother. It's up to me to make sure they don't have to endure a similar loss."

"Oh, I see. This is for *them.* Is that why you were going to marry me?" she asked carefully. "For the boys?"

His tone became a tad defensive. "Well, you *are* great with them. And they're crazy about you."

"And?"

He deliberately chose to misunderstand her. "They like me, too—but with you here, I wouldn't have to worry about them when I'm away."

"And?"

He bristled. "Well, hell. We get along better than a lot of couples. And you've got to admit—the sex is great."

"Ah. Is that what I get out of it? Great sex?"

He was starting to look uneasy at her ultrareasonable tone. "That's part of it, sure. But you'd also get the kind of family you never had as a kid. Plus, you'd get all of this." He made a sweeping gesture that encompassed the pool, the house, the grounds, his gaze snagging momentarily on the cabana behind her. "You wouldn't have to worry about money," he said, lowering his voice fractionally as he brought his gaze back to her. "Hell, you wouldn't have to work if you didn't want to. I'd take care of you."

"How...kind of you." She began to tap her foot. "Let me see if I've got this straight. You were going to give me money and a roof over my head and allow me to vicariously relive my childhood through your kids. And, as a bonus, you'd take me to bed whenever you dropped in. And all I had to do in return is stay home and devote myself to you and the boys. But then I went and screwed things up by risking myself over some stranger's child, thereby proving I can't be trusted to keep myself safe for you and them."

He had the grace to flush at how it sounded when she put it that way, but he refused to back down. "It's more complicated than that, and you know it—but yeah. I guess that pretty much covers it."

"Well, you know what I think, Alex? I don't think this has a darn thing to do with the boys. They weren't the ones who were all shook up down at the Mini-mart."

"So what do kids know? They don't have the sense to be afraid when they damn well ought to be."

"*Exactly*." She paused for the space of a heartbeat and added pointedly, "But that isn't true with adults, is it?"

A muscle ticked to life in his jaw. "What are you getting at?"

"I think *you're* the one who's scared. You said it yourself. When Allison died, you went from having a 'perfect' life to having 'nothing'—except loneliness. And you've worked hard to keep it that way. Lord knows, most people would get down on their hands and knees and be grateful to have health, wealth, great looks and three bright, beautiful children—but not you. You've spent four years keeping everybody away, and I think it's because it made you feel safe. Because you can't lose what you don't have, can you, Alex?"

"You don't know what you're talking about!"

"Maybe not. But I still think the reason you're angry is because you finally figured out you care more for me more than you thought, and it scares the hell out of you!"

"Oh, yeah? Well, think again!" he said furiously. "I thought a tough reporter like you dealt in facts, not fiction!"

Shay's temper finally snapped. "You want facts? I'll give you facts! Fact one—I'm not afraid to admit when I care about someone! Fact two—I'm not too proud to own up to a mistake, even when it's a whopper—like falling in love with you! And fact three, which is last, but not least—the only way I'd marry you is if you got down on your knees, professed your undying love and—and kissed my feet, you pigheaded fool!"

"Are you finished?" he shot back.

"Not quite!" Without further ado, she shoved him into the pool. "*Now,* I'm finished." And with that, she turned on her heel and walked away.

Women! Alex thought furiously, as he stalked across the patio, his shoes squishing with every step. *You couldn't trust them! Let your guard down for a second and there was no telling what demented thing they'd do!*

He stormed into the mudroom and began to strip off his clothes, a drill that was becoming disgustingly familiar. So much so that he had his shirt half off before he remembered Mrs. Rosencrantz was back. Well, great! He could just imagine her reaction if he popped through the door in his underwear. He'd be lucky if all she did was quit!

With a muttered curse, he stalked over to the door and peeked around the frame. There was no sight of the housekeeper, but the boys were sitting at the counter, eating. Again.

"Aren't you guys ever full?" he growled.

They glanced over at him, their faces the picture of innocence. Brady raised an eyebrow. "What?"

"Oh, don't give me that," Alex said impatiently. He sent them a shrewd, knowing look. "I saw you lurking in the cabana, eavesdropping. I ought to send you all to your rooms for a month—without food."

"Gee, Daddy—" Brady began.

"Forget it," Alex said irritably. "Where's Mrs. Rosencrantz?"

"It's her night off," Nick reminded him.

"Yeah," Mikey said. "That's how come Brady said we needed to go see you by the pool." He looked guilelessly at his older brother. "Isn't it, Brady?"

At Alex's snort, Brady glared at his little brother. "Thanks at lot, Mikey." He turned his gaze back to his father. Since he no longer had to pretend, he said bluntly, "So did you and Shay kiss and make up?"

Alex tugged off his shirt and dropped it to the floor with a wet splat. "No."

"Well, when are you going to?"

"I don't know that we are." He yanked off his shoes, scowling at the pathetic condition of the formerly butter-soft leather. Chlorine clearly didn't do a thing for handmade Italian loafers.

"What!" Brady jumped up so quickly his stool toppled over.

Alex skinned out of his pants. Clad in nothing but his boxers, he walked over, snagged a clean dish towel out of the drawer and scrubbed at his hair.

"But you've gotta make up!" Brady said shrilly. "How are we going to get Shay for our mom if you don't?"

"Gee. I don't know," Alex said sarcastically. He bent down and scooped up his soggy clothes. "Maybe we'll have to pass on *that,* too." He headed for the hall, the boys dogging his footsteps like tails on a kite.

"But you can't!"

"Oh, yes. I can."

"But—but—what are we going to do?" Brady wailed as they all arrived at the door that led to the basement. "We need her!"

"I don't know about you, but I'm going to go put my clothes in the laundry," Alex said, deliberately misunderstanding. He switched on the overhead light, then relented somewhat as he took in all three boys' stricken expressions. He sighed impatiently. "Look, don't worry about it, okay? We'll talk about it later. I promise."

"When?" Brady demanded.

Give the kid an inch and he thought he owned the ruler. "Tomorrow," he said firmly.

"But, Dad—"

"The subject is closed for tonight." Alex turned and tramped down the stairs, refusing to respond any further.

Brady was undeterred. "We'll see about that!"

Yeah, right, Alex thought, making his way toward the utility area. He'd had all he was going to take of people telling him what he should do, feel or think.

Take Shay for example, he thought, as he flipped up the lid of the washer, poured in a cup of detergent and tossed in his clothes.

Where the hell did she get off, trying to make him feel like a heel for wanting to marry her! Since when had offering to share all your worldly possessions with a woman become an insult? Would she have liked it better if he'd asked for a prenuptial agreement?

And as long as he was on the subject, how come it was so wrong of him to place a high value on her relationship with the kids? Wasn't *she* the one who was always talking about how great they were? And how lucky he was to have them? Hadn't *she* thought less of *him* before he took a more active involvement?

And what about all that psychoanalytical mumbo jumbo about him being afraid to care for anyone too deeply? After all, he loved his kids, didn't he? Sure, he'd been gone more than was wise the past few years, but then, a man had to earn a living. And he'd been here the past few weeks. Why, if he'd listened to *her,* the boys would be off at some adolescent boot camp, learning how to invade foreign countries or something!

And as far as his feelings for her went, what the hell was so wrong with...*like?* Maybe it wasn't love, but the concern he'd felt when she'd gone chasing after that car at the Mini-mart had been real enough. The idea that she might fall and have the life squashed out of her had appalled him. Hell, he hadn't felt that helpless, that frightened, that furious, that distraught, that *devastated* since—

Since Allison died.

The thought slammed into him, nearly knocking him off his feet. He clutched the edge of the washer, oblivious as he knocked the entire box of detergent in. Shaking his head, he told himself harshly he'd made a mistake.

The entire idea was ridiculous. Ludicrous. Impossible. Of course he hadn't felt as strongly today about Shay as he had about Allison. He'd *loved* Allison. He'd loved her the first time he'd seen her, when she'd come to work at the Olympiana the summer they'd both turned twenty. It had been instant, effortless, uncomplicated.

Not at all like what he felt for Shay. What he felt for Shay was deep and complex. It was as bright as one of her smiles, as intense as the passion she stirred in him, as vibrant and dynamic and multifaceted as her personality.

That wasn't love.

Or was it?

He took a deep breath. God knew, he was no longer the easygoing, uncomplicated youth he'd been that long-ago summer, he thought slowly. Nor was he even the man he'd been four years ago, when he'd foolishly thought he had the world at his fingertips and that he was invincible.

Life had left its stamp on him, and not all of it was for the better. In the past month alone, if he hadn't been difficult and ungrateful, it was probably because he was too busy being insensitive and self-centered.

And Shay loved him, anyway. She'd given him her warmth, her laughter, her heart. And what had he offered in return?

A chance to share his bed and be an unpaid nanny.

He gave a groan of self-disgust. It was probably a miracle she hadn't shoved him in the pool a lot sooner.

The most dangerous thing I ever did was fall in love with you, you fool.

The question was, what was he going to do about it?

Before he had time to decide, footsteps thundered overhead. Frowning, he wondered what the hell was going on now. If the boys were sliding down the stairs in empty pizza boxes again, he swore he was going to—

"Alex?" A woman's frantic voice floated down the stairs, growing louder as the footsteps approached. "Oh, boys, thank goodness! Where is he?"

It was Shay. He slammed down the top of the washer and turned on the machine just as Brady said from the top of the stairs, "Daddy's down there!"

"He's really bad!" Nick added.

"Hurry," Mikey exhorted.

Like the answer to Alex's prayers, she appeared at the top of the stairs, her expression agitated. "Where?" she asked, looking frantically around as she started down.

Alex leaned back against the washer, folded his arms, and tried to look calm.

The boys exchanged a look, retreated like smoke sneaking up a chimney and slammed the door. There was an audible click as the bolt shot home.

"What the—" Shay spun around. "Brady? Nick? Mikey? What the—"

"I believe this is what's known as a setup," Alex said, stepping forward.

She turned around. "Alex! Oh, Alex! You're all right! I thought—the boys said—but actually you look—" She stopped, her mouth gaping a little as she took in his attire—or lack of it. "You look...*fine*," she accused.

"Thanks. So do you." She was barefoot, in shorts and a barely-there T-shirt as usual.

"But Brady called and said—ooh!" Color suffused her face. "That little liar!" Her eyes narrowed ominously, she swiveled, marched back up and pulled on the doorknob.

The door didn't budge.

She slapped her palm against it. "Brady! Open the door! Do you hear me?"

There was an instant of silence. And then Alex's eldest son said distinctly, "No. We took a vote. We're not letting you out. Not until you and Daddy make up!"

"It'll be a cold day in—" She cut herself off. A tremor went through her shoulders as she fought for control.

"He sounds as if he means it," Alex observed.

She was *not* going to turn around. She *wasn't*. Not when he was down there looking gorgeous, with his hair boyishly mussed for once and his clothes God knew where. Not after she'd made a major fool of herself, telling him how he felt, pushing him in the pool, confessing she loved him.

She slapped the door again. "Brady!"

"I don't know where he gets that stubborn streak," Alex went on. "It must come from his mother's side of the family. Of course," he said thoughtfully, "Beau can be a little obstinate. And James has been known to dig in his heels—"

She swiveled around. He'd moved to the foot of the stairs. She glared at him. "Don't just stand there babbling in your underwear, Morrison. Do something."

He gazed up at her, something in his expression that she couldn't define. "First, I have a question," he said quietly.

"Can't you find something to put on?"

"How come you're here?"

She bristled. "Because. Your sons called and said that you'd fallen and you needed me. Not that I cared what happened to *you*," she added hastily. "I came because I thought *they* needed help."

They both knew she was lying.

He walked up the stairs. He was three shy when he confounded her by dropping to his knees. He leaned forward, closed his fingers around her ankle and pressed a whisper-soft kiss to her bare instep.

"Alex! Have you lost your mind? What are you doing?" she asked, clinging to the railing for balance.

"I'm kissing your feet," he informed her.

"Why on earth—"

"Because my sons are right. I *do* need you. And because you said the only way you'd marry me was if I got down on my knees, professed my undying love and kissed your feet. So I thought I'd start with the hard part and—" he pressed a second kiss to the side of her arch "—work my way up."

"Alex—"

He released her foot and stood. "You were right," he said quietly. "About...everything. I am a jackass. But I love you, Shay. More than anything. I'll do whatever you say—give up the business, sell this house, stay home full-time while you work, whatever you want. Just say you'll spend the rest of however long we both have left with me. Marry me. Please."

"Oh, Alex...yes."

He pulled her into his arms and held her pressed to his heart. For the second time that day, she could feel him trembling. After a moment he raised his head. "Brady? Nicholas? Michael?"

"What do you want, Daddy?" Hope laced Brady's voice.

Alex winked at Shay. "We've decided to kiss and make up, but there's a condition."

"What's that?"

"You have to give us ten minutes alone."

There was a hurried consultation. "Well...okay. But you guys have to talk about us getting married."

Shay and Alex smiled at each other. "It's a deal."

There was an instant of stunned silence, and then Brady cried, "All ri-ight!" and all three boys began to jump up and down and cheer.

Shay gave a startled yelp of her own as Alex scooped her up in his arms and swept down the stairs. "Where are we going?" she asked, pressing a kiss to the taut ridge of his collarbone.

"There's a bed down here somewhere," he murmured, nuzzling her neck.

A slight movement caught her eye. She glanced idly over his shoulder.

Brutus was poised atop the washing machine, which was ominously spewing bubbles.

Shay smiled and decided she'd wait awhile before she said anything to Alex—at least ten minutes. Instead, she closed her eyes and sighed happily as his mouth claimed hers, bestowing a kiss filled with promises as they reached the bed.

It didn't get any better than this.

Epilogue

Dateline: August 5

To: Beau Morrison
    Correspondent, World News International
      Magazine
    c/o Moscow News Bureau
    Micromini cassette No. 4

Hey Uncle Beau, I think the wedding was perfect, don't
you? The pool looked real pretty with all those flowers
and candles floating on it, I really liked the fountain
cake, and Grandma cries the best of anybody. You and
Uncle James looked nice, and I thought it was pretty
cool the way me and Nick and Mikey had suits just like
Daddy's. But the very best part was when Brutus got
loose and the singer lady fainted and fell into the pool,
and the fire-and-rescue guys had to come revive her.
Now, that's a wedding!

It was sure good to see you. And me and the guys really like the African drums you brought us. Daddy says to tell you that someday he'll return the favor. He also says to say thanks again for the ring. He still can't believe it only cost $9.42!

Oops, I gotta go, Uncle Beau. The limo is here to take us to the airport to start our honeymoon and *my mom* is calling me!

I *always* do what she says because she's the best.

Love from your happiest nephew in the whole wide world— Brady.

P.S. You know, now that I've got a mom, I could really use an aunt and some cousins. I've been thinking...

* * * * *

SILHOUETTE® Desire®

COMING NEXT MONTH

#943 THE WILDE BUNCH—Barbara Boswell
August's *Man of the Month,* rancher Mac Wilde, needed a woman to help raise his four kids. So he took Kara Kirby as his wife in name only....

#944 COWBOYS DON'T QUIT—Anne McAllister
Code of the West
Sexy cowboy Luke Tanner was trying to escape his past, and Jillian Crane was the only woman who could help him. Unfortunately, she also happened to be the woman he was running from....

#945 HEART OF THE HUNTER—BJ James
Men of the Black Watch
Fifteen years ago, Jeb Tanner had mysteriously disappeared from Nicole Callison's life. Now the irresistible man had somehow found her, but how could Nicole be sure his motives for returning were honorable?

#946 MAN OVERBOARD—Karen Leabo
Private investigator Harrison Powell knew beautiful Paige Stovall was hiding something. But it was too late—she had already pushed him overboard...with desire!

#947 THE RANCHER AND THE REDHEAD—Susannah Davis
The only way Sam Preston could keep custody of his baby cousin was to marry. So he hoodwinked Roni Daniels into becoming his wife!

#948 TEXAS TEMPTATION—Barbara McCauley
Hearts of Stone
Jared Stone was everything Annie Bailey had ever wanted in a man, but he was the one man she could *never* have. Would she risk the temptation of loving him when everything she cared about was at stake?

MILLION DOLLAR SWEEPSTAKES (III)

No purchase necessary. To enter, follow the directions published. Method of entry may vary. For eligibility, entries must be received no later than March 31, 1996. No liability is assumed for printing errors, lost, late or misdirected entries. Odds of winning are determined by the number of eligible entries distributed and received. Prizewinners will be determined no later than June 30, 1996.

Sweepstakes open to residents of the U.S. (except Puerto Rico), Canada, Europe and Taiwan who are 18 years of age or older. All applicable laws and regulations apply. Sweepstakes offer void wherever prohibited by law. Values of all prizes are in U.S. currency. This sweepstakes is presented by Torstar Corp., its subsidiaries and affiliates, in conjunction with book, merchandise and/or product offerings. For a copy of the Official Rules send a self-addressed, stamped envelope (WA residents need not affix return postage) to: MILLION DOLLAR SWEEPSTAKES (III) Rules, P.O. Box 4573, Blair, NE 68009, USA.

EXTRA BONUS PRIZE DRAWING

No purchase necessary. The Extra Bonus Prize will be awarded in a random drawing to be conducted no later than 5/30/96 from among all entries received. To qualify, entries must be received by 3/31/96 and comply with published directions. Drawing open to residents of the U.S. (except Puerto Rico), Canada, Europe and Taiwan who are 18 years of age or older. All applicable laws and regulations apply; offer void wherever prohibited by law. Odds of winning are dependent upon number of eligible entries received. Prize is valued in U.S. currency. The offer is presented by Torstar Corp., its subsidiaries and affiliates in conjunction with book, merchandise and/or product offering. For a copy of the Official Rules governing this sweepstakes, send a self-addressed, stamped envelope (WA residents need not affix return postage) to: Extra Bonus Prize Drawing Rules, P.O. Box 4590, Blair, NE 68009, USA.

SWP-S795

He's Too Hot To Handle...but she can take a little heat.

SILHOUETTE

Summer Sizzlers

This summer don't be left in the cold, join Silhouette for the hottest Summer Sizzlers collection. The perfect summer read, on the beach or while vacationing, Summer Sizzlers features sexy heroes who are "Too Hot To Handle." This collection of three new stories is written by bestselling authors Mary Lynn Baxter, Ann Major and Laura Parker.

Available this July wherever Silhouette books are sold.

MEN OF THE BLACK WATCH

a new series by BJ James

Meet Jeb, Mitch and Matthew, three mysteriously sexy
bachelors—and the women who are destined to learn
their every secret.

They're three agents—members of the secret
organization, the Black Watch—and they've sworn
to live by a code of honor. Now they're faced with
the three toughest assignments of their lives.

In August—
Jeb must betray the only woman he could ever love.
HEART OF THE HUNTER (#945)

In September—
Mitch meets the woman who will melt his tough heart.
THE SAINT OF BOURBON STREET (#951)

In October—
Matthew risks his heart for the woman he promised to
protect. **A WOLF IN THE DESERT (#956)**

Only from

As a *Privileged Woman,* you'll be entitled to all these *Free Benefits.* And *Free Gifts,* too.

To thank you for buying our books, we've designed an exclusive FREE program called *PAGES & PRIVILEGES™.* You can enroll with just one Proof of Purchase, and get the kind of luxuries that, until now, you could only read about.

*B*IG HOTEL DISCOUNTS

A privileged woman stays in the finest hotels. And so can you—at up to 60% off! Imagine standing in a hotel check-in line and watching as the guest in front of you pays $150 for the same room that's only costing you $60. Your *Pages & Privileges* discounts are good at Sheraton, Marriott, Best Western, Hyatt and thousands of other fine hotels all over the U.S., Canada and Europe.

*F*REE DISCOUNT TRAVEL SERVICE

A privileged woman is always jetting to romantic places. When <u>you</u> fly, just make one phone call for the lowest published airfare at time of booking—<u>or double the difference back!</u> PLUS— you'll get a $25 voucher to use the first time you book a flight AND <u>5% cash back on every ticket you buy thereafter through the travel service!</u>

SD-PP3A

𝒯REE GIFTS!

A privileged woman is always getting wonderful gifts.
Luxuriate in rich fragrances that will stir your senses (and his). This gift-boxed assortment of fine perfumes includes three popular scents, each in a beautiful designer bottle.   <u>Truly Lace</u>...This luxurious fragrance unveils your sensuous side. <u>L'Effleur</u>...discover the romance of the Victorian era with this soft floral. <u>Muguet des bois</u>...a single note floral of singular beauty.

𝒯REE INSIDER TIPS LETTER

A privileged woman is always informed. And you'll be, too, with our free letter full of fascinating information and sneak previews of upcoming books.

𝑀ORE GREAT GIFTS & BENEFITS TO COME

A privileged woman always has a lot to look forward to. And so will you. You get all these wonderful FREE gifts and benefits now with only one purchase...and there are no additional purchases required. However, each additional retail purchase of Harlequin and Silhouette books brings you a step closer to even more great FREE benefits like half-price movie tickets... and even more FREE gifts.

L'Effleur...This basketful of romance lets you discover L'Effleur from head to toe, heart to home.

Truly Lace...
A basket spun with the sensuous luxuries of Truly Lace, including Dusting Powder in a reusable satin and lace covered box.

Complete the Enrollment Form in the front of this book and mail it with this Proof of Purchase.

PROOF OF PURCHASE
Offer expires October 31, 1996

SD-PP3